'John Bingham, having made one name for himself as a writer of cunningly engineered murder stories, is now turning to espionage . . . Mr Bingham juggles with the options in an atmosphere of treachery, blackmail, and assassination. In the precisely drawn island setting he builds up the plot like the master craftsman he is, and the end comes with a nice unexpected twist.'

Daily Telegraph

'Mr Bingham puts situation and surroundings to his reader exactly as one wants to know them. You get Cyprus politics in an understandable way. You get just the right touch of topography. You feel at ease and, because you do, you feel with the hero uneasy . . . like grubby old illogical life.' *The Times*

Also by John Bingham in Panther Books

My Name is Michael Sibley
Five Roundabouts to Heaven
Marion
A Fragment of Fear
I Love, I Kill

John Bingham

Vulture in the Sun

Panther

Granada Publishing Limited
Published in 1973 by Panther Books Ltd
Park Street, St Albans, Herts

First published in Great Britain in 1971
by Victor Gollancz Limited

Made and printed in Great Britain by
Richard Clay (The Chaucer Press) Ltd
Bungay, Suffolk
Set in Linotype Times

A Note

The Communist Party of Cyprus is phonetically known as AKEL, and I have spelt it as such, though technically it should be written A.K.E.L., because the letters stand for different words: ANORTHOTIKON KOMMA ERGAZOMENOU LAOU, which can be translated as the Reformed Workers Party.

Similarly, the National Organisation of Cypriot Combatants is phonetically known as EOKA, and I have spelt it as such, though technically it should be written E.O.K.A., the letters standing for ETHNIKI ORGANOSIS KYPRION AGONISTON. This was the underground armed force during the struggle against the British.

ENOSIS is a single word meaning UNION—in the Cypriot sense, union with Greece.

VOLKAN is a Turkish word, meaning volcano, one of the underground Nationalist Turkish armed groups.

London, 1971. J. B.

Chapter One

Much later, I was to say to Ducane that a plastic bomb, even a small one, can kill you, like a bullet, and probably will, and it can also mutilate you and blind you, and he was to say, well, well, you're still alive, aren't you, so in a sense the affair has a happy ending and I would say, bitterly, it all depends what you mean by a happy ending. But that was still some time ahead.

Meanwhile, I was pretty tensed up, and doctors say that's bad.

There are various ways of removing tension, and with a view to following medical advice I put my arm round her shoulder so that her head was raised, and lifted her slightly from the warm sand, and bent my own head towards her. She raised her face almost imperceptibly—lips parted, eyes closed, and all that.

How you assessed her physically depended on your mood.

If you didn't want to make love to her, she was tall for a woman, with big bones, lethargic in movement, not light.

If you did want to make love to her, she was of medium height, with slim bones, graceful in movement, and voluptuous, full bosomed, with a slim waist and good thighs.

I did want to make love to her.

I was surprised that she reciprocated, in the circumstances. Very surprised. She seemed to guess my thoughts.

'This is not love,' she said. 'I'm not falling in love with you. This is just physical.'

'Blame the sea and the sunshine.'

'This is animal stuff,' she pointed out after a few minutes.

'Some animals are luckier than other animals,' I said. 'Lucky animals are killed before they are eaten. Others are just eaten.'

'You don't need to kill me.'

She caressed the side of my face.

When I had eaten her I lay back relaxed and lit cigarettes for both of us, thinking there was often much to be said for the medical profession. Neither of us spoke.

She finished her cigarette, buried the end in the sand, for she had tidy habits, and said she was going for another swim. I said I wouldn't accompany her. I was still digesting the meal. I have noticed that women seem to recover from meals more quickly than men. In some ways they are physically the stronger sex, and need to be, and they live longer. Good luck to them.

I watched her walking across the sand, noting the movement of her hips, and the light brown of her skin against the white swimsuit, and saw, beyond, the Mediterranean blue and mauve and dark red, and how the coast line stretched, dark and rocky, past Akhiropiitos Point to distant Cape Kormakiti and the lighthouse.

They call Cyprus the Island of Aphrodite, Goddess of Love. This mid-day was the first taste of love I had encountered here, except that it wasn't love. The word was a euphemism. She had been right.

She wasn't in love with me, of course, and I certainly didn't love her at that time. I didn't even know if she was a friend or an enemy. In the muddied water of treachery I wasn't now sure of anything. A nice state of affairs indeed.

I watched her in the water, swimming out to sea with slow strokes. She was a fine animal all right. There was no harm in having a passing snack. Or was there?

I edged back into the shadow of a boulder, out of the noon sun, lying on my side, and traced in the sand with my forefinger the crude outline of an Argonaut warship, thinking I had never wished to come to troubled Cyprus in the first place.

Chapter Two

The outline of the job, as described by Ducane, had reeked of death and destruction, and of despair and failure. It still did, in spite of the sea and the sun and the snack I'd just had.

The trouble was, and always would be, that it was almost impossible to say no to Kenneth Ducane. It is also almost impossible for some people to refuse certain challenges and live with self-respect. Ducane knew that.

He knew too much, that guy. It's fine when a colleague knows too much about other people, it's interesting and amusing. But when he knows too much about you yourself, and what makes you tick, you don't cheer so loudly, not always, you don't.

I had had enough mental stress and tension in recent months to last me a lifetime, and I guessed if I went to Cyprus there would be more. I didn't want to be depressed. I wanted happiness, to see it around me and be conscious of it.

I knew that the Greek Cypriots and Turkish Cypriots had been at each other's throats. I had read of the turmoil and mutual killings and the burning of houses, and though the United Nations troops were now there, temporarily separating the two communities, there only had to be a major incident to set off a civil war, then a major war.

When it came to Cyprus, I just didn't want to know, and when Kenneth Ducane mentioned Cyprus I told him so. But when he switched on the charm, and the smile spread across his fawn-coloured face, making it look curiously like a friendly frog, I groaned silently knowing my resistance was doomed. I tried a last defence.

'Cyprus is a friendly country—why spy on Cyprus?'

Ducane looked astonished.

'Certainly it is a friendly country—and we don't spy on it. So is Turkey, Turkey is an ally, a bastion of Western defence in the eastern Mediterranean. So is Greece. In whose interest would it be to weaken or destroy the Western defence system in those parts? Who would like to see Greece and Turkey at war? Go on, tell me.'

But I did not reply.

'We don't spy *on* them, we spy *for* them. It's only a temporary assignment,' he said insidiously. 'Lovely weather in spring, more of a holiday than anything else. Just filling in, to help Frank Baker get some long leave. He needs it. A long rest.'

He was looking thoughtful. He added, 'Frank doesn't think he needs a rest. And he thinks the island can't do without him. Both are bad signs. Let's leave it at that. He's got some woman friend in Athens, but Athens is a long way away.'

He picked up some papers on his desk and tossed them across to me.

'Glance through that lot. And think again before you turn down the Cyprus job, you being what you are.'

I didn't ask what me being what I am meant. I thought he might tell me, but I noted the light challenging tone and was again aware of a feeling of defeatism. I was tired, and if I wanted to go anywhere it was to the Yorkshire moors, windswept and clean, and filled with memories of my boyhood.

I took the papers and stared at them miserably. Ducane said acidly:

'We, the British, getting thrown out of Cyprus was a triviality, a passing if painful incident in the dissolution of an empire. This is more important. You should know that Mr Ben Cullon, mentioned by Frank Baker, is a Canadian hotelkeeper in Kyrenia. He owns the Thessides Hotel. He is in effect an agent, though unpaid, a man of good will, Frank says. Frank often uses his hotel. He is staying there now.'

I shook my head and pushed the papers back towards him. He ignored them.

'Look, I'm not interested.'

'Afraid?'

'Afraid of what?'

'Yourself,' he said coldly.

'Yes,' I said, and sighed, and picked up the papers again.

They were reports from Baker which had been translated from cypherese into some semblance of English. I handled the first report with as much enthusiasm as I would have done if it had been impregnated with radio-active fall-out. It read:

'Report begins. Mahmoud Kadem, under his cover of a Turkish business man, has made progress in his secret negotiations with the Cypriot government in Nicosia for a settlement of the Greek–Turkish differences in the island, and flies in four days' time for confidential talks in Athens. He then returns to

Istanbul. We must hope for the best. Tension remains high in the island, and the slightest incident could set the two communities fighting again, this time with almost certain intervention from Turkey, fifty miles away, and all the inevitable and disastrous repercussions from the Greek mainland.

For obvious reasons I have not had direct contact with him, but Ben Cullon, of the Thessides Hotel, where he is staying, reports that Kadem, who trusts him, has told him that he believes he is under some sort of surveillance, and has expressed apprehension. Cullon told him that the surveillance was doubtless a form of discreet protection initiated by the Cypriot authorities.

Kadem replied that he was unconvinced, and so, in his heart, is Cullon, I think, because he told me that he has felt that he himself is under study, and he is sure it is not by the Cypriot police. I will not detail the various small incidents which have led him to this conclusion.

I will only add, for what it is worth, that for the first time I believe some attempt was made last Thursday to gain access to the safe where I keep certain essentials, including cash for agents. The combination lock withstood the attempt, and the device which openly reacts to indicate that unauthorised entry has been attempted or is being attempted may well prevent further intrusion. The disturbing thing is, however, that access to my flat, obtained via my business below, was made without damaging either the office door locks, or those of my flat, or the windows.

There is only one set of keys, which I carry with me, though there are obvious occasions—when going for a swim, for example—when I am separated from them. I have, of course, had the door locks changed, and re-set the combination lock.

Report ends—Orpheus.'

I handed the paper back to Ducane. He said:

'Here is another report received this morning.' It read:

'Report begins. Mahmoud Kadem was today in a state of optimism. He confided in Ben Cullon that his "business" talks, as he calls them, have been progressing reasonably well, that he flies to Athens soon, and that much is involved which could not be to the advantage of "people interested in keeping Turkey and Greece as enemies".

Report ends—Orpheus.'

'Frank will fill in the picture for you when you arrive,'

Ducane said blandly, and hesitated. 'I don't encourage flights of fancy from officers in the field, as you know, but I suppose you might as well glance at Frank's views on vultures.'

He sniffed and looked disapprovingly at the file in front of him.

'What vultures?'

He flicked through some pages and said:

'This is a whimsy report from Frank about a month ago. I'll read the final paragraph. "There is a vulture hovering over this island, and it is not one of the native birds. Of that I am convinced. His location, of course, is not yet known to me. The vulture, as you know, does not normally kill his own prey, but profits by the slaughter of others. And this vulture, while depending hopefully upon the Turkish–Greek issues for possible future food is, I believe, periodically interested by other cross-currents which could yield eventual carrion. It is these other cross-currents which worry me, largely because they are as yet intangible. I believe that Ben Cullon senses something in the air. He refuses to admit it, but he has been more thoughtful, less high spirited, of late. Perhaps the feeling I have had of being under some sort of observation, in various public places, is due to my imagination. Maybe I have been too long in the island of Aphrodite, or that I have been at this work too long! Who knows?" '

'Most of us get jumpy now and again,' I muttered.

'He is not the jumpy sort. He's tired, but not jumpy. This was before the attempt on his safe.' Ducane paused, then said: 'If he exists, this vulture, he could be one of many things—an agent working to the Russians, a Turkish agent working to Istanbul and preparing to provoke trouble as an excuse for a Turkish invasion if the talks break down, or an agent working to Athens with the same idea—or he could be a fanatic, a loner, organising a local band of fanatics.'

'Or a gangster,' I said, 'connected with the Mafia, organising —this and that?'

He shook his head and walked to the window, and looked out over Regent's Park to the distant sight of the Zoological Gardens and the Mappin Terraces.

'No, not that, Tom.'

'Sure?'

'Pretty sure. The Mafia hasn't reached into Greek or Cypriot territory.'

'There's always a first time.'

He shook his head again but less certainly, and turned from the window and went back to his desk, muttering:

'Abdul-the-Damned would have had a sniff of it.'

I relit my pipe and said:

'Well, that's fine, that is, I'm relieved to hear that Abdul-the-Damned, whom I've never heard of, would have had a sniff of it. That's a great consolation, that is.'

I flew to Nicosia, Cyprus, thirty-six hours later, mugging up a little Greek mythology on the way. The ancient Greeks went in for brotherly love all right. It wasn't usually a blood brother, because they stopped short of incest. But the Greek gods and goddesses took everything in their stride, sexually. Zeus, and his lot, were a very rum crowd indeed. Most odd.

Even Aphrodite's background wasn't all that hot, as I pointed out to Damon Nicolaides, before he hated me.

Chapter Three

Frank Baker was at the airport when I landed at about 9.30 p.m. I had not met him before. He was tall, about forty-five, going grey above the ears. The rest of his hair was dark and wiry. His face was round, the chin receding very slightly, though I knew this meant nothing. Two of the bravest men I know have receding chins, and three of the soppiest dates I've ever met have square or jutting jaws.

He held himself erect, had a yellow saturnine look about him. I thought he'd probably been a throw-out from a colonial police-force when the Empire folded up, and I was nearly right, because he'd been in the Sudan Civil Service before he landed in Intelligence.

He greeted me perfunctorily when I had passed through Customs. I thought he might have been more friendly, but he seemed to be interested in the crowd awaiting passengers from the plane, friends and relations, porters from hotels, taxi-drivers offering their services, and general hangers-on and lay-abouts with seemingly nothing to do.

A porter took my suitcases. As we followed, Frank Baker said:

'There's a woman over there on the right with a red handbag talking to two other people. Behind her, alone, is a man in dark trousers and a white shirt, no jacket, smoking a cigarette. Have a look at him.'

'Why?'

'It's a long story. Just have a good look at him.'

I did, and said nothing. It was the wrong place for a long story.

I saw a squat individual with heavy shoulders and short thick legs, swarthy, standing rock-still, watching the scene. The only movement he made was when he raised his cigarette to his mouth as we passed. He had a gold ring on the third finger of his right hand.

We got into the car and drove off. The air was very warm, especially after London, where the citizens had been enjoying typical spring weather such as heavy cloud and drizzle and a temperature near freezing point. But I wasn't in much of a mood to enjoy the warmth. I didn't want to be where I was, and I hadn't much liked my reception when I'd arrived where I was.

Frank Baker was driving a big Rover, and he said hardly a word till we had left Nicosia airport. At one point, his mind on something else, he absentmindedly took a wrong turning in the dark, and I heard him swear softly. We were passing through a ruined suburb before he found his tongue in a stilted way.

'Used to be a prosperous Turkish community. Look at it. Houses wrecked. Burnt. Both. Looted, of course. Doors and window-frames gone, too. Lot of killed and wounded. Just before Christmas. Peace on earth, goodwill, all that boloney. Makes you sick.'

He was right. Trim, neat little houses in which families had taken a pride. Remains of well tended gardens. All now lonely and desolate. It did make me sick, and was one reason why I hadn't wanted to come.

'You suggesting the Greek Cypriots are the only ones to blame?' I asked.

'Course I'm not,' he said irritably. 'The Turks are bloody obstinate. Can't forget they ruled before the British. Want more power than their numbers warrant. Demands about municipalities, police, law courts, the lot. Some of them want partition. You'd think they wanted apartheid or a Mason-Dixon line.'

'I wouldn't think anything,' I muttered, 'I'm just a new boy.'

He was driving very fast. I'm no slouch at the wheel, but I wouldn't have taken some of the bends in the villages on the Kyrenia road as he did. I reckoned I had been correct, Ducane wrong. Frank Baker was jumpy all right. It doesn't make for good driving.

We passed out of the Greek zone round Nicosia. The way to Kyrenia was through an agricultural Turkish zone. Once or twice a Turkish soldier stepped out of a red and white striped sentry-box and signalled him to slow down. Frank took no notice. I suppose he had faith in a British car and a British number-plate as a passport of neutrality.

I didn't. I always expected to hear a bang and the splintering of the rear window, and bent forward and lower in my seat. But nothing happened. The old Turk, whatever his faults, is a tolerant, easy-going chap.

Suddenly he stopped the car outside a Turkish inhabited village. There was no sign of life. A dog barked then was quiet. Everybody was probably in bed. Life was not gay in a Turkish zone.

Frank Baker got out of the car, saying, 'Sniff some air.' It sounded like an order.

We stood by the side of the road, looking up at the stars, and I sniffed. There was a lemon grove at hand, and some flowering shrubs. He was right. It was worth a sniff. After a few seconds he said abruptly:

'Love this bloody island!'

The way he snarled the words out you'd have thought somebody was extracting a confession at the point of a gun.

'Love the people, too. Want to knock their heads together. For their own good. Different cultures, different histories. Still, ought to be able to sort things out. Kadem's hopeful. Got the right personality. Splendid fellow. Leaves tomorrow, thank God. Morning plane to Athens.'

'Tomorrow?' I said, surprised. 'I thought he wasn't due to go for a couple of days.'

'Things speeded up. Weight off my mind when he goes. Tell you that. Afraid he'd be bumped off. Lot of people would like it. Very dangerous yesterday and today. Nearer to Greek–Turk agreement, nearer to assassination. That's my view, that's my view in the present circumstances. Very dangerous tonight, too. But I've got plans.'

He was standing erect, stiff as a ramrod, gazing out at some fields on the side of the road opposite to the lemon grove. I heard him mutter again, 'Love this bloody island, love its people,' and remembered the report in which he had said, surely wanting to be contradicted, that maybe he'd been on the island too long, maybe in the Service too long.

Perhaps he had. I formed the impression that he was over tense and bordering on the neurotic. He seemed to have the wrong impression, that he was personally responsible for Kadem's safe arrival in Athens. Because he loved the place, and because Mahmoud Kadem represented the best chance for peace, he had got involved to a degree far beyond the call of duty. That's what I thought. He swung round and said accusingly:

'Giles Brewer knew the set-up, he could have come out. Not that I need leave.'

I said sulkily, 'I'm not responsible for what Ducane decided, and what's more I didn't want to come here. I didn't wangle this trip, you know.'

I had hardly spoken the words when I knew I was in trouble. His back seemed to stiffen even more.

'Indeed? So Cyprus isn't good enough for you? What posting did you want? Paris? Berlin? Brussels? Fat living and no work?'

He certainly was neurotic. He certainly needed long leave.

I said nothing. I know these near-nut cases.

Whatever you say gets twisted. Best to keep your trap shut. I turned my back on him, took a step or two along the road and began to fill my pipe, and guessed he was watching me. Suddenly he did a complete *volte face*, and I wasn't surprised. These people often do.

'Sorry,' he said quietly. 'Very rude of me. Didn't mean it. Got a bit nervy lately.'

I raked up a phoney hearty laugh and told him to forget it. I said I wasn't surprised he was on edge. London thought he was doing a wonderful job. Ducane was delighted.

Di-da-di-da-di-da.

I almost believed what I was saying.

He did, anyway. I could see the tension seeping out of him.

'So Ducane's pleased, eh?' he purred. I expected him to start washing his face with one paw.

'Says you're irreplaceable,' I lied.

'It's nice to know one's small efforts in odd corners of the world do not go unappreciated,' he murmured, and led the way back to the car.

From then on he was normal, except for an outbreak near bedtime, but that wasn't directed against me.

'The man you asked me to look at when I arrived, what about him?' I asked, when we had got going in the car again.

'Spiros Artaxides, a thug. You know the general political position?'

'Roughly,' I said, whereupon he went on to explain it as though I'd said I didn't know the set up. There was the ENOSIS crowd, he said, who were disappointed when the end of British rule hadn't meant complete union with Greece. There was EOKA, which had been the terrorist arm of ENOSIS when the British ruled. It was disbanded, but was lurking, and could be revived by extremists. There was AKEL, the official Cypriot Communist Party, and there was VOLKAN, a secret Turkish terrorist organisation equivalent to EOKA. Like EOKA, it still lurked. VOLKAN people had killed EOKA people. EOKA people had killed anybody, British, Turks, Greeks, Greeks friendly with the British, and sometimes each other.

'There's the rest, the majority, ordinary Cypriots, Greeks, and Turks. Don't give a damn,' Baker said bitterly. 'Want to live in peace. Did under the British. Could do again, if Mahmoud Kadem has his way.'

He was back to the Kadem syndrome.

'Spiros Artaxides,' I said to head him off. He took a curve in a Turkish village, tyres screamed, and I winced.

'Corners beautifully, this car. Let you have it while I'm away.'

'When are you going away?'

'When? Didn't Ducane tell you? Tomorrow, of course, to start with. With Kadem. Got a contact in Air-Athene. Booked a seat behind him. Deliver him safely, job completed. Relax in Athens a couple of days. Maybe three. Maybe more. Then come back here for a bit, then go on long leave. Don't need it, don't need it at all, and things are dicey here. But Ducane insists.'

He hesitated, then said abruptly:

'Got a friend in Athens. More or less engaged to her. Haven't told the office. Tell you in confidence. Fine young woman.'

'Congratulations, you're lucky. Is she Greek?'

'Half.'

I waited for him to go on.

He had the opening, but he didn't. I left it at that. It was not for me to intrude into his Athenian pleasures.

'Spiros?' I said, after a few seconds. 'Chap at the airport?'

'Small fry, engineer. Cretan, used to be in AKEL. Resigned a year ago. Came under social-democrat influence. Said events had overtaken theories, Communism all washed up. Long live the Cyprus government and Makarios, and all that. Interesting case of man mellowing with years. Very interesting.'

I said nothing. I was a new boy. Such things do happen. Now and again. But not often.

He pointed to the Kyrenia range of mountains on our left where, high up, pinpoints of light showed.

'Fort St Hilarion. Connected with Richard Coeur de Lion, Crusaders and all that. Long history. Occupied by Turks now. Dominates the pass on the Nicosia–Kyrenia road.'

I nodded, still thinking of Spiros Artaxides. We had left the

Turkish zone and were approaching Kyrenia. Street and house lights were struggling against the moonlight, and the moon was winning.

'Entering the Greek zone,' Baker said briefly as two khaki-clad figures carrying rifles stepped into the road by the check-point.

'They know my car, I expect,' he said, and drove at them without slowing down.

One day he'll do it once too often, I thought as we went through, and hoped some other guy—perhaps Giles Brewer, whom he was so keen on—would be with him instead of me. Aloud I said:

'That Spiros character, he may have reformed politically, but he looked like a thug to me. What the Yanks call a hood. It was his build and the way he stood—motionless and intent.'

'He was a thug, a Cretan thug, in EOKA. That's all over.'

'He still looks a thug to me,' I muttered.

'You don't want to go by looks in Cyprus. Lots of them look like retired brigands, especially in old age.'

'This one looked as though he wasn't retired.'

'You don't want to judge by appearances,' he insisted, with a touch of his old irritability.

Poor old Frank Baker.

He could hardly have been more wrong if he'd tried. And in view of what happened later, he must have tried very hard indeed from time to time.

But I agreed at first with his assessment of Ben Cullon and his wife, Marion. He gave me a quick run down on them before we arrived at the hotel. They'd come to Cyprus because Marion had bronchial trouble and needed warm winters. Been on the island about eight years, two years longer than Frank. Ben Cullon had good contacts among Cypriot government people and the Turkish leaders. Both sides trusted him, used his hotel. Mahmoud Kadem was staying there now. Ben Cullon had been useful to Frank in the matter of recruiting agents. It sounded reasonable as he outlined it.

Marion Cullon was at the reception desk when I arrived. I thought she was probably French Canadian. You could see a French strain in her dark hair, olive skin, lively brown eyes and well kept figure. Frank Baker introduced us. She greeted me like an old friend, as did her husband when he came out of his office a few moments later. They were the sort of hotel proprietors you feel at home with at once, and the warm feeling lasts, at any rate until you get the hotel bill.

Ben Cullon was tall and slim, with a thin face, a straight nose and blue eyes. He had a slight scar on one side of his face, between the left eye and the nose, the result of a bad car accident. At the age of about thirty-eight he looked like a matured Greek god, and had one of those crushing hand-shakes which make you wish you'd kept your distance and just bowed a greeting. He pressed me to have something to eat, but I'd had a plastic meal on the plane, and anyway it was getting on for eleven o'clock and I had a date with Frank Baker in his room.

I thought there'd be a good deal to discuss.

If there was, he'd slashed it to the bone. As he said, it was only for a few days, but it was the briefest and most unsatisfactory hand-over I'd ever experienced.

He poured out coffee and Cyprus brandy, lit a cigarette, unlocked a drawer, and handed me a large-scale map. The map had crosses and numbers written on it in ink.

'Rendezvous places,' he said briefly. 'Attached to the map are pieces of paper with map references and further explanations for each place. Cross-roads, clump of four carob trees, cart tract, lemon grove, big grey rock, and so on. Can't go wrong.'

'Not if you say so, I suppose.'

'I do say so.'

He took out his wallet, took out a slip with some names, addresses, code names, and telephone numbers on it, and handed it to me.

'Agents,' he said starkly. 'Tell you about 'em.'

There were only three names. I wondered what he had been doing with his time in the last six years. He saw the surprised look on my face, and said: 'Lot of other contacts, of course. You don't need details. Keep 'em in here.'

He tapped his wallet.

'Keep 'em all in here since the attempt on my safe. Let you have them when I get back.'

I was appalled, but I said nothing. The abandoning of all our professionalism, of all security technique, of all rules governing the security of agents and contacts was so complete that I now, for the first time, began to wonder whether Frank Baker was not merely tired but suffering from some serious mental deterioration.

I had accepted his brusque, erratic manner and speech, but to carry a list of his agents and contacts on his person pointed to eccentricity bordering on a mental breakdown.

I was wondering what had caused it—Cyprus brandy, Cyprus weather, or both—when he began to explain the names.

'First name, Ahmet Aksu,' he said, and took a swallow of the thin brandy. 'Code name, Vizier. Keeps a Nicosia shop. Sells postcards and tourist trash. Used to come to this hotel before the trouble. Ben suggested him to me. Member of VOLKAN terrorists. Probably doesn't tell us everything. Better than nothing. Don't press him. Gets obstinate. Be grateful for small mercies. Due for payment tomorrow.'

He took a white envelope out of the drawer. 'Twenty pounds. Call if you can. Shop near St Sophia Mosque. Address on that list.'

He was sitting upright in the chair now, head raised, as if he were listening for something. After a while he relaxed, said:

'Second name on list, Damon Nicolaides, code name Apollo, former Communist agent in AKEL.'

'Former?'

He looked annoyed at the question.

'That was the word used—expelled from the Party six months ago. Alleged ultra Left Wing pro-Maoist tendencies. Balderdash. Trumped-up charge. Doesn't know why. Nor does Ahmet. VOLKAN has a line into AKEL, but VOLKAN doesn't know.'

I could have made a guess, I could have asked him whether he'd got careless over the years, besotted with Cyprus conditions. He said:

'Nice lad. Got to know his father, widower, through Ben Cullon, then Damon. Idealistic chap. In love with a Turkish lass called Selin something. Hopeless here, of course. Out of the question. Dangerous even. Romeo and Juliet stuff. Plans to go to America.'

The staccato voice stopped.

He paused and looked thoughtful. He's been slugging the brandy, and maybe it had softened him up, because when he continued his words were less jerky, his speech almost fit for human consumption, except that now there was a touch of the Sudan Civil Service in his voice and manner. He leaned back in his chair, held the lapels of his jacket, gazed up at the ceiling, and began intoning as though to a departmental secretary.

'I have promised to help with the American authorities,' he said impressively. 'I think it right and proper to do so. This individual has assisted us materially for four years. He will be expected to fill in certain forms and to answer questions, for instance whether he has been a member of certain organisations such as the Communist Party. A negative answer would carry obvious risks. An affirmative answer could prejudice his chances of obtaining American citizenship, should he so desire. I have one or two personal contacts with the Americans and these I propose to utilise and to indicate his true role for us in the Cypriot Communist Party.'

He could have been writing a ponderous Minute in a file to a superior officer. All that was needed was: 'For approval, please.' He seemed to be addressing himself to himself rather than to me. Reassuring himself. Visualising another Minute back, 'Approved. I leave the timing to you.'

I solemnly gave my unwanted approval and nodded.

'It is a rehabilitation case,' he said earnestly. 'He helped us, we help him. That is right and proper.'

I nodded again. I couldn't at that time imagine anything which need cause us to break our word. Faithful servant rewarded, and all that. I was still inexperienced in some directions.

'The last one on the list, Saleh Karim, is a curious fellow,' he said. 'Code name Zeus. I think of him as Abdul-the-Damned. Lebanese chap. Small import–export business in Beirut and Famagusta. Courier for us. Sometimes brings back bits and pieces from a head agent over there. Coded, of course. Nothing at all urgent. Small stuff. Urgent stuff goes over the air.'

He added that anything brought over in the next few days could probably await his return. He could have saved his breath, I'd already decided that. He poured out another cup of coffee, added a slug of brandy, and said casually:

'He makes money on the side smuggling lost and stolen passports into Beirut.'

As a throw away line I thought it good.

'British ones, too?'

He seemed surprised at the question.

'Certainly—British, French, German, the lot. Somebody will do it anyway. Better Karim than somebody we don't know.'

He saw me trying to puzzle out the subtlety of the argument.

'He marks them, see? Small perforation mark behind the photo. And supplies me with a list. There is a marginal advantage in seeing where some of them land up. You haven't been very well briefed in London, have you?'

He looked at me resentfully.

'I haven't been briefed at all, Ducane said you'd do it yourself. Don't bother if it's too much trouble,' I added acidly. 'I'm just temporary, that's all.'

'Sorry.'

I noted the neurotic switch again, from the aggressive to the humble.

'Saleh Karim is paid three hundred American dollars a month. He had a predecessor who was paid one hundred and fifty, and disappeared.'

'Disappeared?'

'On a boat journey from Famagusta to Beirut. Saleh Karim said the incident was worrying. He said he would be less worried if he himself was paid three hundred. So he gets it, and doesn't seem to be worried any more.'

For a moment I thought hopefully that he was trying to be amusing in a sardonic way. But he was staring at me seriously enough. Suddenly he sat upright, listening for something again, like a watch-dog. I expected to see his ears become erect and elongated, and waited for a low growl. Footsteps were outside. Then the sound of a door opening and shutting opposite.

'Communications?' I asked, not knowing what had bitten him. 'Communications with London in case of emergency?'

He didn't answer. I might as well not have been there. He got up and opened the door, then closed it three-quarters, sat in his chair, got up again, opened it a trifle more, sat down again, and seemed satisfied.

'Mahmoud Kadem, the Turkish representative,' he muttered. 'Going to watch his door all night till he leaves. Guard against an inside job. Deliver him safely to Athens. Job then done. Relax for a few days.'

He was back in the old personal responsibility groove. It wasn't a few days' relaxation he needed, it was a few months. Perhaps more. He had taken a small bottle out of a drawer and shaken two blue tablets out of it. I watched him swallow them one by one, washing them down with a mixture of cold coffee and brandy.

'Drinamyl,' he muttered. 'Keeps you awake.'

'Communications?' I asked again, urgently.

I felt that he was slipping away from reality into some over-dramatic dream world of his own, as a schizophrenic subject might do.

He looked at me impatiently, reluctant to switch his gaze from Mahmoud Kadem's bedroom door.

'What about communications? Alex Ford, five minutes walk from here. Coding and decoding, receiving and transmitting. Knows you're acting for me. Told him. Good man. Formerly Royal Engineers attached to King's African Rifles. Major, retired. Address in here,' he added, and tapped a portable safe. 'Money in here, too, five hundred pounds, not that you'll need it. Nothing much in the safe in my Nicosia flat. Not while I've been here. Can't trust the Nicosia place. You know somebody tried to open the safe? I suppose they told you *that*, at least?'

'I know.'

'Rum do,' he muttered, and drew a chair up to put his feet on.

He was clearly settling down for the night on a self-imposed vigil which to me seemed both futile and dangerous. Futile, because I guessed the Cypriot Special Branch police would be keeping a watch on the outside of the hotel, and Ben Cullon would be able to vouch for his inside staff. Dangerous, because on my way out Frank Baker asked me to switch off the room light, which I did, leaving him with the table drawer open and a Walther automatic inside the drawer. If Frank Baker happened to nod off, and if Kadem rang for room service, and Frank suddenly woke up and saw the waiter, then the waiter's insurance company, if he had one, was likely to suffer a setback.

But I said nothing.

I went to bed thinking of the drinamyl tablets. There are better pills available to us in the Service to keep us awake on a job. Drinamyl will help, but drinamyl tablets are primarily anti-depression pills.

I wondered what he had to be so depressed about that started him off on drinamyl.

I don't need much sleep, which is just as well. Doubtless with some idea of getting the new boy's nose down to the grindstone at once, he'd fixed up a busy day for me.

Early the next morning, at eight o'clock, I drove him in his Rover to Nicosia airport. We arrived half an hour before the plane was due to leave. He filled me in a little more on the jobs he wanted me to do in his absence. There was nothing much to them.

Call on Alex Ford and make my number.

See and pay Ahmet Aksu, our Turkish agent in VOLKAN.

See Saleh Karim and take anything he had. This was an easy one, he said, because Karim called openly at the hotel, being friendly with Ben Cullon, and I could give him coffee and brandy in my room.

The only other job involved some rehabilitation work for Damon Nicolaides. Damon Nicolaides was due for his fortnightly meeting with his girl Selin that morning. It was all supposed to be very secret. Frank had organised an elaborate set-up. Nicolaides was picked up at a street corner on the outskirts of Nicosia and driven to a spot between Larnaca on the coast and the Tekke of Hala Sultan. Here he would disappear into the woods along a disused track to some undisclosed spot known only to him and Selin.

Meanwhile Saleh Karim was doing his stuff, earning part of his salary, by picking up Selin on the outskirts of Famagusta and ferrying her to the far end of the disused track, where she too disappeared into the woods. What happened when Damon and Selin met in the woods was left by Frank to my imagination.

Admittedly it is the custom of Ducane's mob to provide a sort of after-care service to agents who have worked well for us. This is good and proper. But the whole of this operation, especially the use of Saleh Karim, seemed to me highly unprofessional, unnecessarily complicated, and typical of a Secret Service officer who had been in the field too long and had too little to do.

Saleh Karim allegedly knew nothing of the object of his taxi work. I thought, if you can believe that, you can believe anything. However, I was just a temporary, and if they wanted to vamp up these cockeyed high jinks locally, it was none of my business. I wasn't interested. I hadn't wanted to be there in the first place.

I kept my trap shut.

Ten minutes before the plane was due to take off a big white saloon car drove up and stopped about twenty yards from where we were parked.

'That's him—Mahmoud Kadem,' muttered Frank Baker.

A short, sturdy figure in a dark suit, carrying a briefcase, got out of the car, followed by two men in sand-coloured suits whom I guessed to be plain-clothes police officers. Frank Baker grabbed his suitcase. I accompanied him as far as the barriers permitted and wished him a good journey.

His face was radiant, in spite of sitting up all night. He looked at his watch.

'Job completed in a couple of hours! God, I'm relieved.'

He seemed to have grown ten years younger. I reckoned he was already thinking of his girl in Athens. He was suddenly relaxed and easy and fit for human consumption, and the whole neurotic Mahmoud Kadem fixation seemed to be draining out of him.

'Don't get sky-jacked,' I said facetiously.

He laughed, but he gave me a serious answer.

'I've checked the passenger list and the crew. No Arabs, no Jews, no extremist Greeks, no extremist Turks, no unfriendly people.'

I believed Frank Baker. He had told me he had a good contact in the Cypriot police, via Ben Cullon. He was right, too. There was no hostile agent among the plane crew or the passengers. Nobody at all unfriendly. Agents try not to commit suicide.

There was merely a bomb on board.

It lay cold and emotionless, inert in its plastic container, dormant, slumbering until the aircraft reached twenty thousand feet, then awakening slowly to life, then stirring more rapidly as the air pressure got further to work, until in the end the air pressure became intolerable to it. And it protested in the only way it could.

Suspecting nothing of what was in the womb of the plane, I gave Frank Baker a cheerful final wave. I was glad for him that his worries were over. They certainly were.

On the way out, standing back a little from the taxis and porters, motionless, half-hidden by a pillar, was the ex-Communist who had seen the light, Spiros Artaxides, former member of AKEL, the Cypriot Communist Party, the extremist who had mellowed and turned social democrat.

I have a beady eye. I spotted him before he spotted me.

When he saw me he turned aside and pretended to consult his watch, turning his face from me. I wondered whom he was waiting for this time. Or whether he was seeing Frank Baker off, or Mahmoud Kadem. Or both. And why.

She stayed in the sea for about half an hour. I joined her for the last ten minutes, and we floundered and floated and porpoised about in-shore, and then ate the packed lunch and drank half a bottle of wine. Like all packed lunches it relied on hunks of bread with very little butter, but there were a few pieces of meat and goat's milk cheese hanging around somewhere, if you could find them; and an orange and a banana to deceive you into thinking you were having a Belshazzer of a feast.

But it didn't make us sleepy, at least not at first. We had another animal snack, owing to the sea and the sun. This time she did the eating. She didn't kill me first, but she seemed to do her best. I got the impression she hadn't had a snack for a long time before she met me.

Then we did get sleepy. Before she nodded off she said again:

'Don't get any funny ideas. I'm not going to fall in love with you.'

'Suits me okay,' I murmured drowsily. 'I'm not falling for you, either. I've got other things to do.'

'I'm glad you didn't say better things to do,' she said, and gave a sort of half-laugh:

'I guess it was a slip of the tongue.' I stroked her forearm to take the sting out of the words. I liked her body and her low, pleasant way of speaking. If she had a job to do, I couldn't see what it was. Maybe she expected me to blab things out, one day, like Frank Baker had done. But for whose benefit?

Maybe I was wrong, you get an instinct, and sometimes it's right and sometimes it's wrong. And you get suspicious of dollies who seem easy.

Looking back on it, her approach had been a bit melodramatic. I hoped like hell I was wrong. I raised myself and looked down at her long legs, lightly dusted with sand now, and her full figure.

As I said, I liked her low, pleasant voice.

Chapter Four

The agent network was ridiculously small, it seemed to me, and to cram it all into one day seemed unnecessary. Still, it would leave me plenty of free time later to wander about seeing the island. That's the sort of nutty thing one does think sometimes.

I picked up Damon Nicolaides in a Nicosia side street without difficulty. All I had to do was sit in the car until he came up to it. He knew it well enough, since it was Frank's car. We exchanged the usual recognition words, and then we were away, out of Nicosia and across the Mesaoria plain, where the wheat and barley crops grow studded with red corn-poppies, the wild yellow chrysanthemums and pink convolvulus grow, each flaunting its own gentle gaiety.

Here and there, perched above the road like trappers' log-cabins, were the little United Nations outposts, bravely flying a blue flag, trying to keep an uneasy fragmentary peace more by their presence than by what they were empowered to do.

As we neared the spot where I was to drop him, he said that anything could happen in Cyprus because Cyprus was the birthplace of the goddess Aphrodite, who was beautiful and in her day so powerful. And who knew for certain what lingering influences might or might not remain?

I looked round at him quickly, and then jerked the wheel to avoid a bump in the road.

He was twenty-six, slimly built, with the usual brown face and brown eyes of a Greek Cypriot. What was unusual was the blond hair. Somewhere along the line there must have been true ancient Greek blood from the mainland, or else a nordic strain.

'There are more things above us and around us than we know of, as your poet said,' he added, in his careful English accent, and smiled.

'Well, Aphrodite had bad blood,' I said, and looked round again at him. He was still smiling.

'Bad blood? What is meant?'

'You want to look at her ancestry.'

He thought for a moment, then said:

'Her father was the great god Zeus.'

'Zeus! And who were *his* parents?'

'The god Cronus and the goddess Rhea.'

'And who was Cronus son of,' I asked, glad that I had mugged up my mythology. He paused then said quickly:

'The god Uranus and the goddess Gaea.'

'And who was his wife Rhea the daughter of?'

'Uranus and Gaea.'

'So Zeus, father of Aphrodite, was the son of a brother and sister marriage?'

Damon Nicolaides fielded that one easily.

'Brother and sister marriage was not unknown in those days. The same was found in Egypt among the Pharaohs.'

I changed down to third gear, then to second, then to first, to weave my way through some goats.

'Zeus married a goddess called Hera, so Aphrodite their daughter——'

'Aphrodite's mother was not Hera,' Damon interrupted, falling into the trap.

'So Aphrodite was illegitimate?' I pointed out triumphantly.

'Things were different in those days,' Nicolaides said and laughed, clearly enjoying the cut and thrust. I think he had a sneaking feeling, even a subconscious wish, that the power of Aphrodite might still linger somewhere in the land, but he also had a sense of humour. He was reluctant to leave the subject, and said:

'Aphrodite's father was Zeus, but her mother was a sea nymph called Dione. Although born in the water, as you know, Mr Carter, she rose from the sea—*Aphros* meaning foam, and *dite* meaning sent, as you also well know, sir, having clearly studied these grave matters.'

'I'm sorry for Hera. After all, when the great Apollo, son of Zeus, was born, and his daughter Diana, too, who was the mother of these children? Not Hera, not likely! Old Zeus had strayed again, not with a sea nymph this time but with a new love, Leto, and no wonder Zeus once had to turn Leto into a quail to escape Hera's revenge. Poor Hera, I'm not surprised she grew bitter.'

Nicolaides remained silent for some seconds. Then he said:

'There is another story connected with the birth of Aphrodite. I do not like it. Uranus, father of Cronus, was wounded in battle by Cronus, and his blood fell into the sea near Cyprus, turning the water and foam all pink, and from this bloodied sea Aphrodite arose in her beauty. I do not like the story,' Damon Nicolaides said again, and stared sombrely ahead.

I said nothing. I also did not like the tale.

On the left of the road I slowed down by a lemon grove, and on the edge of the road, at one end of the grove, by a big carob tree, I stopped the car. Between the lemon grove and a wood of mixed trees a little-used, partly overgrown stony path led away from the highway. It was so narrow, so little frequented that it was, in effect, not so much a path as a way along which men occasionally went to tend the lemon grove or strip it of its fruit.

I turned to Nicolaides. His eyes were shining with excitement. I leaned across him and opened the passenger door for him, and patted him on the shoulder.

'Off you go. I will pick you up in exactly two hours.'

I watched the slim figure of Damon Nicolaides, ex-agent in AKEL, the Cypriot Communist Party, disappear round a bend in the path. He was not going now to some secret political meeting. A Greek Cypriot, he was going to a love tryst with a Turkish Cypriot girl, which at that moment in history was much more dangerous.

So I watched him go and wished him well.

I thought, Cyprus is the land of Aphrodite, and Aphrodite is the goddess of love, and Aphrodite rose from the bloodstained sea, and it was a strange way for a goddess of love to be born, and if, as Damon liked to imply, some of her influence might remain in the island, was it a good thing? She was born in a bloodstained sea. Blood had been spilt in Cyprus, Greek Cypriot, and Turkish Cypriot, and, if what Ducane had said was right, there might not only be new blood in the sea but upon the earth and in the streets, starting red and quickly drying to brown in the hot Mediterranean sun.

In the distance I saw the cyprus trees near the Tekke of Hala Sultan and made towards them, feeling suddenly jaded and sickened by man's hatred of man, desirous of a place where I might find peace of soul, if only for an hour or so.

The road to the Tekke of Hala Sultan ran between forest trees towards the Salt Lake. The guide books said that 'many attractive walks may be enjoyed through the forests and by the Salt Lake'. This was currently unlikely, since the area was alive with United Nations troops, lying in the shade of their armoured vehicles or encamped among the trees. I passed some Danes who had taken off their blue berets and were relaxing. They gazed idly at me as I drove slowly past. They looked bored stiff.

The Salt Lake had a curiously unreal air about it. The water was not blue, but was of a muddy, pearl colour over which the late morning heat shimmered.

Tall rushes and bamboos grew round the edge, and on the far side birds were wheeling. I stopped the car and got out. The air was still and there was no near sound, and I had the impression that I was looking at the setting for a Chinese painting, and thought again of Aphrodite rising from a bloody sea. And I listened to the silence, and instead of peace of soul I felt an unreasonable sense of loneliness and depression.

Damon Nicolaides was with his Turkish sweetheart, perhaps in some secluded corner surrounded by the little wild cyclamen sparkling like jewels, and though the present times were perilous those two were young and had their future on which to pin their hopes.

It was different for me.

I began to walk slowly along the road, filling my pipe. In the silence my footsteps sounded impersonal, as though I myself were walking noiselessly, disembodied, and some other man, some stranger, were making the sound on the roadway.

I stopped and lit my pipe, and the click as the top of the lighter snapped into place was companionable. But when the silence closed in again, I turned abruptly round and made my way back to the car, because in the car I would know I was alive and not a spirit wandering by the side of a mirage.

'You're daft as a brush,' I muttered aloud, and inserted the ignition key. 'You want your ruddy head examined, you do.'

Further down the road a khaki-clad Greek soldier, hardly more than a schoolboy, stepped out of a blue and white sentry-box carrying a rifle. I slowed down, but the boy just looked at me sullenly and made no move to stop me.

At the gate to the Tekke another young Greek stopped me. I pointed to the mosque, disused since the troubles.

'Will you show me around?' He nodded, and we walked along the dusty road. The Greek said:

'This is a Turk place. Mahomet—his half-mother is buried here.'

He didn't spit at the mention of Mahomet's step-mother, but I thought it was a near thing. He opened a sun-faded wooden door set in an archway under a red tiled roof. Inside, the garden surrounding the mosque was deserted and overgrown with weeds. I knew that since the communal troubles no Turks were allowed in to tend it. Hala Sultan had the misfortune to have been buried in a Greek Cypriot area. But if the Greek soldiery barred access to Turks they were also there to prevent desecration of the tomb by Greeks.

Hala Sultan, it was written, 'broke her pellucid neck' when she fell from her horse during an Arab invasion of Cyprus. The garden around her mosque was now unkempt, but at least she still slept in peace, pellucid neck undisturbed by intruders.

The fretted door of the mosque was locked, the huge padlock rusted on its hinge. The shrine and garden were silent, except for the sound of flowing water.

'The Turks are pigs,' the soldier said.

He pointed to a fountain and added disapprovingly,

'They wash their feet there, before going inside.'

'Can I go in?'

'You cannot see the main tomb without a permit. There are others.'

The other tombs were behind the mosque, plain slabs with large stone ornaments on top, shaped like chimney-stacks, tombs of a warrior race, looking like martial cloaks topped with tarbushes.

I glanced briefly at them and turned to go back, listening to the gentle water which flowed around the garden in narrow channels between dry-stone edging, dripping from one level to another, still keeping the deserted garden fresh, sweet and green. The mosque cupola was silhouetted against a postcard-blue sky. Now and again a faint breeze stirred the slim black cypress trees.

I walked ahead of the soldier, along a path paved with pink flag-stones, part of which led underneath a great vine, noting the lemon trees and scarlet flowering pomegranates, and loquats already on the ground, seeking to establish within myself the tranquil peace which the garden offered me. But my depression grew deeper. It was as though I knew of the plastic obscenity in the belly of Frank Baker's plane which only a miracle could have sent to sleep again, and which a miracle hadn't sent to sleep again. I heard the Greek mutter:

'Pigs—the Turks are pigs, no?'

'If you say so,' I replied wearily.

I picked up Damon Nicolaides by the giant carob tree, and took the dusty Larnaca road to where he wanted me to drop him. A few miles away, if all had gone well, Saleh Karim would have picked up Selin the Turk, and be speeding back to Famagusta, using his Lebanese passport, if need be, to cross the Greek check-points; or any other passport, come to that, of the various ones which he probably had at his disposal, once more regarding the journey as a minor chore to be completed to earn his salary. Damon Nicolaides said:

'In a few months we leave Cyprus, sir. It is decided. I have an uncle in Chicago who owns a dry-cleaning business. He is American, very liberal. I shall join him.'

'And press pants?'

'To start, I shall press pants, sir,' the ex-secret agent said seriously.

'And Selin?'

'She will go to an aunt in England and wait until I can send for her.'

I slowed down and stopped. We were three miles outside Larnaca. Damon opened the door to get out.

'It may take time,' I said gently.

'She will wait for me. She will wait for ever. And I will wait for ever,' Damon Nicolaides said. 'We will both wait for each other, if necessary for always, sir. I will telephone you soon, from a call-box, as usual. Goodbye, and thank you, sir,' he added politely, and got out of the car. As he turned away, he smiled back at me and said again:

'We will wait for each other for ever. You don't believe it, but it is true!'

'If you say so,' I murmured.

'I see you in two weeks, same time and place?'

I was appalled at the mixture of certainty and despair in his voice. Certainty, because to youth hope and certainty are similar, even when the hope depends upon the goodwill of others; despair, because to those in love separation for two weeks is the equivalent of separation for two centuries.

I nodded, not knowing that in the event I would meet Damon again in twenty-four hours. Or how he would hate me then.

I drove into Larnaca for a late quick lunch.

On the harbour front were palm trees, and between the trees were food and drink stalls, covered by awnings supported by four poles. The tables and chairs were painted in different colours, and some were peeling and had slats missing. There was a liner in the bay and other signs of civilisation, such as Coca-Cola advertisements. I chose the cleanest looking stall and sat on the least rickety chair and was served by a shapeless woman in a black dress stretched sketchily over her body like a settee cover which had been washed too often.

She offered me red mullet but I declined it, thinking it an over-rated fish with too little flesh and too many big bones. So she cooked me kebab on a primitive stove, and blue smoke drifted like the smoke from a gipsy fire, reminding me that kebab was invented by a people on the move, Turkish soldiers who grilled noblets of meat on the end of their swords at their evening camp-fires. She served it with chopped chives, shredded cabbage, cucumber and onion, and it tasted good, very good indeed. I began to feel relaxed until a younger woman, also dressed in black, came up and told me she was half Arab, worked in a hospital, had been scalded by a kettle, and had been married to an English sergeant from Leeds, who had been killed in a car crash, and she had a child by him. She showed me the scald mark on her arm and I finished my meal and drove back to Nicosia.

The island seemed to have dissolved into little armed bands holding strips of territory, each defiantly flying its flags, the neutral blue of the United Nations, the pale blue and white of the Greeks, the white and yellow of Cyprus, the red of the Turks with the white crescent.

Arms, hatred, and fear were everywhere. So far it had been child's play, as things go. A few hundred people killed, a few hundred houses destroyed or looted. Some mosques abandoned, the Turkish zones partly blockaded. Check-points, and rough barriers of empty oil drums and sandbags and rubbish. Local tragedy without international catastrophe. That was the score to date.

Next time it would be different, if there were a next time. I began to sympathise with Frank Baker's relief at the thought of Mahmoud Kadem's safe arrival in Athens.

But Kadem was dead by then, though I did not know it.

So was Frank Baker, because the thing in the belly of the Air-Athene plane had already struck back at the high altitude pressure which had annoyed it.

Later, I asked myself if Frank was dead because he was

getting too near the truth, or because he was fortuitously travelling with Kadem. Was it a case of killing two birds with one bomb; or one bird with one bomb deliberately, and the other by chance; or was it all an accident?

But as I drove to Nicosia to see Ahmet Aksu, the agent in VOLKAN, I still thought that all was well with Frank Baker and Mahmoud Kadem.

The centre of Nicosia is a labyrinth of streets. Some shops are holes in the wall, where men weld, make shoes, sell cloth, pots, pans, mounds of fruit, oranges with leaves still on them, loquats, courgettes, strawberries and bundles of herbs. I braked to allow a boy to walk over to a building site bearing small cups of coffee and glasses of water on a tray with a doyley.

Outside a flower shop, the flowers, spilling over into the sun on the pavement, were wilting and sad. Some women tourists, or wives of British army personnel, sauntered along sucking ice-cream cornets. It was hot and humid.

I made for the great building of St Sophia, formerly a Christian cathedral, now, and since many a long day, a Turkish mosque, and parked the car in a side street near the mosque, and looked at my watch, and sauntered about for five minutes, and at twenty-five minutes past three precisely entered a small shop in the Turkish zone which sold cheap paperback novels in various languages, trinkets, and postcards.

A notice said the shop would be closed at three-thirty, and would not re-open for the rest of the day. There was little to sell, owing to the blockade, and what there was could not attract many tourists.

Outside, the street was pot-holed for lack of materials to repair it.

I flipped through one or two paperback novels, waiting for the only other customer to leave. When he had gone, Ahmet Aksu closed and locked the door and turned to me with an expressionless face.

'He wanted some cartridge paper to draw on, he is connected with the Turkish museum.'

Ahmet Aksu led the way into a small room at the back of the shop, and poured out two cups of coffee. Frank had told him about me.

'We have no paper to draw on,' Ahmet Aksu said stolidly. 'The Greek pigs say that drawing paper is strategic material and therefore is banned to the Turkish zones.'

He paused, coffee pot in mid-air, and added: 'Maybe they don't *say* it, how could they say it? But if they don't say it, somebody *says* they say it. The result is the same. We have no paper to draw on.'

'When do the next Turkish Red Cross ships arrive?'

'The end of June. They bring clothes and food. They don't bring drawing paper. The Greek pigs think we shall leave if they make things bad enough. They are wrong. We shall swelter it out.'

'Sweat it out,' I murmured, sipping the coffee. Ahmet Aksu nodded.

'Sweat it out. What has a beginning must have an end.'

'But what end?' I asked. He shrugged.

'Does it matter? If it is going to happen, there is nothing we can do to stop it—so why worry? If it is not going to happen—why worry?'

I looked at him and thought that physically we had much in common. We were both in our middle thirties, of medium height, well built, with thick ankles and wrists, and had grey eyes. We both had touches of grey in our hair; but while Ahmet's hair was black and coarse above a grey face, I had brown hair and a sallow complexion. I put down my cup and laid a white envelope on the little table between us.

'Your expenses for the month,' I murmured.

He nodded and left the envelope lying on the table. There are certain decencies to be observed in these matters. One did not say, 'Here's your dough—what do you know?' And Ahmet knew he should not eagerly grab the envelope.

'The Turkish representative has left,' I said at length.

'So I hear.'

'We must hope for an agreement.'

It was a platitude but it kept the conversation alive.

'In VOLKAN all hope for a just agreement,' he said carefully.

'And if they do not think it just?'

He shrugged.

'What will be will be,' he said evasively, and added in a low voice: 'There is not only VOLKAN. There is something new. We have certain friends and have heard something. Not much. Something. There is a new organisation. It has guns.'

'EOKA revived?'

'Not EOKA,' Ahmet said firmly. 'Smaller, much smaller, perhaps only a dozen men, perhaps more, perhaps less, but very small.'

'Greek Cypriots?'

'Mostly, not all. Maybe a Cretan, who knows?'

'Maybe a Turk?' I stared Ahmet in the face, and smiled slightly. His face was blank. He did not return the smile.

'Who is behind it? You have an idea? Any idea?'

'If I had I would tell you,' he said softly, and casually removed the white envelope from the table to his pocket.

He would, I thought, he hasn't produced any worthwhile information for months, and he needs the money. This Frank had told me on the way to the airport. But producing no information meant he hadn't invented any. Now he had produced some, not much, but something, and made no grandiose claims about it. Therefore I believed him.

'When will you know more?'

Ahmet got up. The room was used as a stock-room. He picked a pile of guides to Cyprus and began to dust them with an old cloth.

'I would have sold all these long ago, but for the trouble. Tourists seem afraid of the Turkish zones.'

He began to flick at other piles of books, disconsolately and ineffectually.

'I may know more in a week or two, or a day or two, some time, who knows? I have a friend who has a friend. Will you bring me some Exinor stomach powder, please. It is hard to find in the Turkish zone now. I have pains caused by worry.'

I nodded and said: 'Trade will improve one day.'

Ahmet Aksu shook his head, flung the duster down, and said:

'Not trade. I have a niece, very young, very beautiful. She is in love with a Greek. She wishes to marry him.'

He looked at me with hot, troubled eyes, standing still and sturdy in his little dusty store-room.

'Such things cannot be. I love my niece but such things cannot be. She will not tell me his name, but I shall find out. He was a member of AKEL. Rest assured, Mr Carter, I shall find out. I have friends who have friends. All Greeks are cowards and dishonest. My niece is beautiful and innocent. So please bring me some powder for the stomach pains.'

'Where does she live?' I asked, and glanced dismally at my pipe, and thought, as if I don't know, as if I darned well don't know. I recalled some words of Ducane: You need good luck in Intelligence. If you can't have good luck you need an absence of bad luck. Great coincidences are rarely good in Intelligence. Occasionally they are a godsend, mostly they are a swipe in the eye.

'Her parents are dead. She lives with my brother in Famagusta,' I heard Ahmet say, and felt no surprise, only a growing alarm and a claustrophobic despair that I was caught in a situation which I could not contain.

'And the Greek boy?' I asked at length.

'Nicosia,' he muttered sourly. The swipe in the eye had arrived.

'Quite a distance apart.'

'Somebody is helping them to meet. Not a Greek pig, and not a Turk, that is certain.'

Outside, in a back street, two women were arguing. I heard a dustbin lid clang. A dog barked. There was silence in the room. The dog barked again. I toyed momentarily with the idea of telling him the truth, appealing to him, speaking of Damon Nicolaides' past services, but I knew it would be useless.

Money or no money, he would stare stolidly at me and tell me to stop Damon Nicolaides meeting his niece or he would quit working for us. Frank had told me not to press him or he would get obstinate. I could not afford to lose him, not now, not now that he was on to something good.

I shrugged and spread my hands in a phoney philosophical gesture.

'What will be, will be,' I said.

'Not in this case,' Ahmet Aksu replied woodenly.

I got up and left openly by the front door, carrying some books from the shop as though I had been buying them.

'Please do not forget my stomach powders,' Ahmet Aksu said, and locked the door behind him.

In addition to the pot-holes, some of the buildings were pockmarked by bullets fired in the communal rioting. I went back to the car and took the road to Kyrenia, thinking again that so far it was all kid stuff, that if the real thing broke out the buildings wouldn't be scarred by bullets, they would be burned shells, Ahmet's books and trinkets charred and twisted, and Ahmet's stomach probably unresponsive to indigestion powders.

A few miles outside Nicosia I pulled in to the side of the road and let the United Nations convoy go by, shepherding

Greek Cypriots from Kyrenia through the Turkish zone which bestraddled the road to Nicosia. It was divided into two parts, the 'fast package' and the 'slow package', according to the speed of the civilian vehicles.

Each was headed by a military police car driven by Danes, the police car flanked by Finnish outriders on motor-cycles, goggled, looking like men from outer space, waving their arms to make other traffic draw into the side of the road, head-lights blazing though the sun was still in the sky.

After the police car came two Canadian scout cars, crews seated low, bedded down behind protective armoured plating, guns mounted, capable of swivelling; then the Greek civilian cars and buses; then two more scout cars, another police car, and the Investigation Car with its radio, ready instantly to spot trouble and report it. It was mostly bluff. The troops could only shoot to protect themselves if attacked. But the bluff was working for the time being.

In the end all might yet be well in Cyprus.

But I didn't think all was likely to be well with Damon, the Greek, and his Turkish love. If love gets in the way of an agent operation, then love must fly out of the window. If it won't fly, it's pushed.

I decided to advise Frank to scrap the Damon–Selin love tryst arrangements, and hoped he'd agree. As he was already dead, he wasn't ever in a position to consider the matter.

The convoy was long past, the Kyrenia mountains were looming above the rising highway, the sentry-boxes on the road were now uniformly painted in the red and white of the Turks, and soon, on the left, St Hilarion was silhouetted against the sky-line.

I still had a nagging worry. First, could there be two sets of lovers, two Greek young men, two Turkish girls, in love in Cyprus? There could. Second, could both couples be so situated that the young Greeks lived in Nicosia and the Turkish girls in Famagusta? Just possible. Third, could it be that in both cases the Greeks had been in AKEL, and the girls not?

Three coincidences, I assured myself, were just two too many, but to take my mind off the matter I suddenly swung left off the main road and took the narrow road up to grim old Fort St Hilarion.

The road was steep, winding precipitously up to the peak

on which the castle stood with the red Turkish flag flying above it. A Turkish soldier showed me round. His pale face was badly shaved, his grey uniform, with red piping, was shabby, his long-barrelled rifle looked cumbersome and old fashioned. He never smiled, but looked sad and disillusioned.

To the Turk, the place was what it had always been throughout history, a garrison barracks. In the former Lady Chapel, originally devoted to Our Lady, the Mother of Christ, were two bunks with rough Turkish army blankets thrown over them.

'The Lady Chapel,' the Turk said at the doorway, 'where the ladies sat away from the gentlemen in church.'

He had got it all wrong, of course, but it was not worthwhile correcting him. From a window I could see some Turkish soldiers walking up the steep path, apparently talking and laughing, carrying bunches of wild mauve antirrhinums like village boys happily and peacefully returning from a day out. The area was bathed in late sunshine and the distant sea was blue along the shore.

Out on the battlements the young Turk suddenly pointed below and said:

'Vulture! It is not allowed to shoot these birds. They must be living to eat up dead animals.'

Down below a huge bird was planing slowly past. The feathers were honey-brown in the sun, and the head was bent earthwards so that from above the head, the repulsive vulture neck, and the cruel beak were not visible.

'She is smelling the earth, she is smelling for blood,' the Turk said, and I nodded, thinking of the curious paragraph in Frank Baker's report about a vulture hovering over the island.

I followed him round, listening to the drone of his voice. I have never found Cyprus all that interesting. It is too rich in history, has been invaded too much. Greeks, Romans, Persians, Phoenicians, Normans, Genoese, Arabs, and Turks, including Hala Sultan with her pellucid neck, have all had a crack at it and in the process have destroyed much of what had been there before.

I didn't find St Hilarion very interesting, either, except for the different levels on which it was built, and the view; and the muttering of the Turkish soldier about the political situation depressed me. As we parted he was still complaining, and with good reason.

'The Greeks will not let us have petrol for our cars or for our machines in the fields, or things to repair our roads, or wood for our houses, or nails, or medicines, or other things, and they keep us waiting two hours in the hot sun at the checkpoints and search our women, but what has been begun must have an end—even with Greek pigs, is it not true?'

'If you say so,' I sighed.

Turks were pigs, Greeks were pigs. I had a vision of the island inhabited by Greek and Turkish pigs, grunting and squealing and rooting among smoking ruins. Eating anything and everything. Eating their own young, as pigs will do. Eating human flesh, as pigs will do. He accompanied me back to my car and said hopelessly:

'Will you sell me a gallon of petrol, please? I will pay twice the price. I have a sick wife in Nicosia,' he added for good measure.

He nodded when I said I had little in the tank, guessing correctly that I, too, was lying.

I drove into Kyrenia and turned right, skirting the little harbour, and drew up at the Heraklion café under the shadow of the old castle, and ordered a soft drink.

A number of small boats lay in the harbour, their masts and yard-arms in the failing light resembling short leafless trees in winter. I did not stay long, though the evening was warm.

The harbour was bringing me no more peace than the Tekke of Hala Sultan. People were standing in groups on the pavement chattering without smiling. I could not understand Greek, and felt lonely and uneasy. Greek Cypriots are lively and gay, but I heard no laughter, and wondered if communal fighting had broken out again somewhere.

I asked a waiter, who hardly spoke English, but he thought I wanted some special kind of drink, so I gave up and drove back to where the Thessides Hotel, white and modern, stood on a small headland. The sun had set but the sea horizon was a startling red, and the rocks and promontories showed jet black, and I recalled Flecker's line about 'the hidden sun that rings black Cyprus with a lake of fire'.

I drove into the forecourt of the hotel and parked the car, noting with dismay that a large bus was already there, and guessed that a package deal of English tourists had descended on the place.

On the seaward side was a patio with small tables and chairs, surrounded by a five-foot wall, illuminated by overhead fairy lighting. Some tourists, still wearing the crumbled heavy clothing in which they had travelled, were drinking, gazing out at the dark sea and chattering.

I was about to pass into the hotel when something seemed to grip my inside and turn it round a couple of times and then fling it down towards my legs as though it were a lump of warm lead, and that's what a few words, uttered by a shrivelled old bag of an English woman tourist, can do to a healthy guy like me. She had said:

'It's a goner, if you ask me—seven hours overdue, that's what it said on the radio.'

A man by her side said: 'Flying coffins, that's what they all are.'

'B.E.A.'s all right. This was a Greek one—Air Athens or something.'

'They're all flying coffins, all of them.'

'B.E.A.'s all right.'

'Flying coffins,' he insisted, 'the whole bloody lot.'

The lump of warm lead cooled, and became cold, heavy lead. I went inside. Marion Cullon was at the reception desk and nodded to me without smiling. She guessed from my face I had heard the news.

She said, 'They're still searching.'

They would be. If they weren't, they'd say they were. It tones down the shock for relatives and friends. I nodded and went on.

I was making my way to the wide staircase when Ben Cullon came out of his small office. He limped slightly, the result of his motor accident. But the limp was almost imperceptible, except when he mounted the last three steps before the hotel door. Then, as I observed later, he would pause, and put out his right hand, and seem to steady himself before he entered the building.

'You heard?'

I nodded. 'Any survivors?'

He shook his head.

'Bits of stuff floating about. Seems to have disintegrated about fifty miles from Athens. You don't survive that sort of thing, buster. Difficult to hoist it in. Poor old Frank, a good guy, bit quick tempered, but a good guy. And Mahmoud Kadem. God knows what'll happen now. Alex Ford rang.

Wants to see you.'

I nodded again, suddenly thinking of Frank Baker purring like a cat when I'd said London considered him irreplaceable. I was glad I'd said it. But he wasn't irreplaceable, and I knew who was going to replace him, at any rate for some time. And I knew another thing, my instinct had been right about Cyprus. It wasn't going to hold any happiness for me.

Pleasure of a sort, but not happiness.

Any man can find pleasure of a sort, such as animal snacks, provided he isn't a cross-eyed, bankrupt, Eskimo dwarf, and even then he needn't despair.

Ben Cullon drifted off, thoughtful and depressed, and I washed and went down to eat a meal I didn't want. I had a couple of aniseed-tasting *ouzos*, fiddled about with some of the over-rated red mullet, and went along to Alex Ford's house and introduced myself.

It was a dapper little white and blue job, with green tiles and a neat garden with a small well-kept lawn surrounded by flower beds.

He was a short plump man of about fifty, bald headed and red faced with faded blue eyes, and he came out to meet me as soon as he heard the click of the wrought-iron garden gate.

He was wearing khaki-coloured trousers, a short-sleeved white shirt, and a yellow silk scarf loosely knotted round his neck. He led me into his lounge and we had a curiously sultry discussion about the air crash and Frank Baker.

A signal had arrived from Ducane, in London, telling me to carry on as best I could. He'd lost no time. I read it without astonishment or pleasure. A second signal informed me that the Turks were playing it cool, whatever they thought, and a successor to Kadem would arrive shortly.

Alex Ford went through the formalities of dismay when speaking of Frank's death. But I doubted if he was feeling much. He was a man who seemed to be retreating ever more into the past. The immediate imperial past was represented by crossed assegai spears and Zulu knobkerries hanging on his walls, and wastepaper baskets made out of elephant legs. He was currently interested in Roman ruins, and he was, he said, devouring a book about Hadrian's Wall.

One felt that before long he would be progressing quickly back to a study of Iron Age hill forts and thence to Stone Age animal paintings in caves.

Frank Baker's death was a tiresome interruption to Alex Ford's way of life.

'The Salamis ruins here in Cyprus are interesting but not a patch on Pompeii or Herculaneum,' he said earnestly. 'But then how could they be?'

'How could they?' I agreed. 'What about signals to London?'

He didn't seem to hear the question, but to be disappearing into another private mist of antiquity. He looked at me accusingly, ignoring my question, and said:

'Cyprus has too few remains of too many races, you understand?'

I nodded patiently and took another run at it:

'What about communications with London?'

'Eh? I do them.'

'I know you do—when?'

He seemed to be trying to peer through a swirl in the mist. He stared at me with his faded blue eyes, and passed a hand over his pink bald head. I swallowed hard and said:

'Radio transmission and receiving times?'

'I stand by for an hour, morning and evening. Nine in the morning, eleven at night.'

'Emergencies?'

'Emergencies—ah, yes! Emergencies. I telephone Athens, they telephone me. We indicate we want to transmit. It's all relayed from Athens, see? Cyprus to Athens, Athens to London—and vice versa, see? I've only got a medium-range set, that's all.'

Any ham radio operator who could thumb through a cypher book could do Alex Ford's job. I got up to go. I thought that I'd been put in charge of a pretty crummy empire: a young Greek who had been expelled from the Cypriot Communist Party and only needed welfare service, a shifty Turk in a Turkish terrorist group, who according to Frank Baker didn't always tell all he knew, a Lebanese Arab who flogged lost and stolen passports, and a cypher clerk and radio operator called Alex Ford who was disappearing back into prehistoric murk. Ben Cullon seemed a sturdy unofficial ally. But he had a hotel to run, he was a busy man.

Alex Ford accompanied me to the garden gate, muttering about Hadrian's Wall and the raids of the Scots which it was designed to curb. He said it was a real turning point in Roman defensive military strategy, because it wasn't just a static Maginot Line concept, it had sortie gates for cavalry and so was an offensive–defensive affair. I tried to look impressed.

'You don't say?'

'A revolutionary concept for the Romans,' he said eagerly. 'Don't just wait standing on a wall—get out and smash 'em before they've reached maximum effectiveness!'

'Interesting,' I said. You've got to say something.

Back in the hotel Ben Cullon intercepted me and said Saleh Karim was on the terrace. He took another look at me and asked if I was tired.

'Not so much tired as thoughtful, I've got a problem.'

'So *you've* got a problem—I've got twenty-two of them.' He waved towards a cluster of tourists asking questions at the reception desk. 'I've had coffee and brandy sent up to your room. I'll tell Saleh Karim to go up.'

I opened the bedroom door to Saleh Karim a few minutes later, and we shook hands, and looked at each other guardedly behind polite smiles.

Chapter Five

I asked him to sit down by the table on which the refreshments were laid out, and ostentatiously locked the door, because Ducane always said that a little play-acting did good, added a touch of drama, made an agent feel he was cared for, even if he wasn't. I certainly didn't care much for Saleh Karim at that moment.

He was of medium height, but must have weighed about seventeen stone. Middle-aged with a large, fleshy face and a double chin. His nose was large and curved, his eyes dark and wary. On the third finger of his left hand were two thick gold rings and on the third finger of his right hand was a gold ring set with a diamond. His shoes were of brown leather with old-fashioned white triangular insets down the sides, and he wore a cream-coloured silk shirt with a yellow tie and a diamond tie-pin. There were creases in the jacket of his pale brown suit where the material strained against the middle button. In contrast with his size, his voice was curiously thin, almost squeaky.

In my imagination I had thought of him as small fry, a Lebanese smart guy on the make, picking up a bit on the side from British Intelligence, flogging stolen passports, acting as taxi driver to Damon's girl because Frank Baker wished it, a sort of Middle Eastern handyman, a cheapskate eager to pick up the fast American buck or the slow English pound, whichever came to hand.

It seemed I had been wrong. Looking at him I judged that financially Saleh Karim was a very well-watered plant, and couldn't see why he should have worked for Frank Baker with all the risks it involved.

We discussed the air crash as I poured out coffee and brandy, but although he made the usual noises of regret about Frank Baker, they seemed to me formal, as Alex Ford's had been, made in the same perfunctory way as a man will lift his hat at a passing funeral procession.

'You want to discuss something, I take it?' I said at length.

Karim shrugged, heaved about as fat men do when making the simplest movements, took out his wallet, and extracted a small sheet of paper. He handed it to me, breathing heavily.

'These are the numbers of passports which go to Beirut tomorrow, Mr Carter. Seven British, three French, three Greek.'

'All marked?'

'All secretly marked, as asked by Mr Baker. May Allah have mercy upon his soul,' he added hastily, and raised his soft brown eyes towards the heavens before taking a sip of his brandy.

'You taking them over yourself?'

Saleh Karim shook his head and looked at me knowingly.

'This time, no. You will understand it is not wise to do the same thing each time. A friend will take them to Beirut.'

'What are they worth,' I asked on the spur of the moment. It was a waste of time to ask.

Karim shrugged gently and spread his hands, and looked at his knees, and I remembered some line in Kipling about a character who 'veiled his eyes, in the manner of one who is weaving lies.'

'Price is always a matter of negotiation. How can I say?' he murmured, and I guessed he could continue in that vein all night. He had nothing further to discuss. He had handed over his list, and now he sat looking at me, like a cautious toad, hands lying along the arms of his chair. I decided to have a dig at him.

'Some of these passports will get into the hands of Arab terrorists who want to flit into a country, plant a bomb, and flit out again,' I said casually, and watched him.

'They are all marked,' he said. 'If I did not do this trade somebody else would do it, as Mr Baker would always point out.'

Although he spoke placidly I saw him do the eye-veiling business and wondered if they were, in fact, all marked. I had a mental picture of him pointing to a particular one in a batch, and imagined him saying in his squeaky voice. 'That one, my Arab brother, is *not* marked. Use it well.'

'I am an Arab,' Karim said. 'The Arabs say that Jews and Christians and Arabs can live together in peace, and only imperialist Zionism must be smashed. That is what the Arabs say.'

He looked at his hands, veiling his eyes yet again.

'I am a business man, Mr Carter. What the Arabs say, what the Israelis say, what the Russians, or the Americans, or even—you will excuse me?—even what the British say, has some truth and some falsehood. But business must go on. Without trade the people starve, so it has always been, so it always will be. Traders see more truth than statesmen or politicians, they deal with both sides, they hear both sides. No?'

I had hardly been listening. He was touching a sore spot with me.

'Israel!' I said impatiently. 'A small sliver of territory surrounded by half-a-dozen Arab countries, some with oil and vast wealth—pouring out blood and money to regain this slip of country! They could compensate the Palestinians ten times over for the value of the land, and re-settle them, and never feel the loss of the money! Between them, they could, they could do that between them, and not feel it.'

Saleh Karim shrugged. His double chins wobbled. Karim said:

'I may see a vase of little or no worth in the home of a very poor man, but because its design and colour please me I offer money, and if the vase is in a position of prominence I offer more than its worth. And if the owner of the house says, "This vase was made by the father of my grandfather," I offer him yet more, though I may not believe him. If in the end I go away disappointed, in my heart I praise the man, even though as a trader I despise him who goes hungry when with a nod of the head he could eat well for many days and buy another vase as good.'

'We're not talking of vases and stuff like that, we're talking of thousands of refugees in misery.'

I refilled Saleh Karim's glass with brandy and added impatiently:

'I reckon if one or two of these oil sheikhs put their hands in their jeans and pulled out a few million dollars the refugees would settle—vase or no vase, great-grandfather or not. Wouldn't you?'

Karim smiled and looked down at his glass.

'Me, I am a trader, Mr Carter.'

After a moment he took out his wallet and extracted a sheet of paper and looked at the typewritten lines on it.

'May I read you something?'

I was tired, I wished Abdul-the-Damned would go home, but I had been tough with him, rude, and Karim was a paid agent of use to the Service. I nodded and got up and walked to the window so that he should not see me suppress a yawn. Behind me I heard the squeaky voice reading, and the poetry of the words overcome the thin tones.

'Every year I shall say to my little son: We shall return, my son, and you will be with me; we shall return to our land and walk there barefoot. We'll remove our shoes so that we may feel the holiness of the ground beneath us. We'll blend our souls with its air and earth.... We'll turn here and there to trace our lives.

'Where are they? Here with this village square, with this mosque's minaret, with the beloved field, the desolate wall, with the remains of a tottering fence and a building whose traces have been erased. Here are our lives. Each grain of sand teaches us about our life.'

His voice faltered and stopped, and I looked quickly over my shoulder, and then out of the window again, and tugged at the Venetian blinds, making a slight noise, to suggest that my back was still turned to him, because I'd seen that his dew-laps were quivering and the piece of paper he was holding was trembling. There was a damned great tear rolling down one fat cheek. So it was embarrassing.

I jiggled with the blind again, and said:

'That's good, that is, is that all?'

He didn't answer, but went on reading in his squeaky, unimpressive voice:

'Do you remember Jaffa and its delightful shore, Haifa and its lofty mountain, Beth shean and the fields of crops and fruit, Nazareth and the Christian bells, Acre and the memory of Al-Jazzar, Ibrahim Pasha, Napoleon and the fortress, the streets of Jerusalem, my dear Jerusalem, Tiberias and its peaceful shore with the golden wave, Majdal and the remnant of my kin in its land?'

I came back and sat down, and Saleh Karim stuffed the crumpled sheet of paper into his pocket and said, 'It is not important, Mr Carter. It is from a book called *The Return Ticket*, by Nasir ad-din-au-Nashashibi. It is not important, I am a trader, but I found it good.'

I agreed, praising its poetic language, but saying nothing more. He left soon afterwards. As he rose to go I gave him the envelope containing his pay for the month, and watched him put it carefully in his wallet.

When he had gone I sat for half an hour thinking about him, drinking two or three more glasses of the thin Cyprus brandy. At one point I got up and stared out at the moonlight and the black rocks and the dark sea, trying to reconcile certain things about Saleh Karim. In the end, I sat down at the table with a pad and wrote:

1. Karim an Arab.

2. Karim sympathetic to Palestinian cause and therefore anti-Israel. Probably sympathetic to *fedayeen*. Palestine Liberation Army, El Fatah, etc.

3. Karim not poor. Wears silk shirts, two gold rings, gold ring with diamond, tie-pin with diamond. Maybe diamonds not real. Maybe they are. He is well fed.

4. Karim marking stolen or lost British passports. Can afterwards be recognised by passport control officers. Having regard to volume of travel, marked passports only useful for snap checks at air-ports, etc. Of ten passports nine probably used by petty criminals of no importance.

5. And the tenth?

Again I imagined Saleh Karim veiling his eyes as he handed it over, saying, 'This one, my Arab brother, is safe, unmarked, and I have not reported *the number.*'

I looked up, watching a fly performing acrobatics around the table-lamp. Round, and up and down, settling for a moment, then away into the room, and back and down and up, weaving an intricate irregular pattern impossible to record.

So it was with Saleh Karim, the general pattern was the same as the fly's, you couldn't track it on a logical basis. Karim was a well-watered plant, he didn't need the money Frank Baker had paid him, the money I now paid him, and although it was handy to him and his friends to know that certain passports could be used with diminished risks why all the rigmorale?

I leaned back into my chair still watching the fly. After a couple of minutes it disappeared into the middle of the room again and was lost to sight. I was accustomed to the fly, it had become, as it were, part of the fittings of the room and when it suddenly reappeared and settled on the back of my right hand I did no more than twist my wrist to disturb it. It did a couple of quick, tight circuits and settled again, nonchalantly rubbing and intertwining its front legs. I ignored it now.

In the same way, had Frank come to ignore the question of why Karim still worked for him?

The problem of motive continued to nag at me. There were other more profitable places for the fly to go to on that warm night. Why come to me? In the early days Karim might have gone to Frank Baker for the money.

But why now? Why the willing little services, such as lifting the Turkish girl Selin to meet Damon? The sort of thing a man might do who was dependent on his pay packet, not a busy prosperous trader.

I tore the sheet of paper I had written on into small pieces and threw them into the wastepaper basket with other rubbish, and went downstairs.

Ben Cullon was still at his desk, doing some accounts. I saw him through the half-open door of his office, and waved to him. He shouted to me to come in and offered me a Scotch. I went in but refused the whisky and began filling my pipe, and said:

'I don't understand Saleh Karim.'

Cullon put down his pen and smiled. It was the end of the day, and he looked relaxed. Blond and slim and sun-tanned, the sleeves of his white shirt were rolled up and he had taken off his tie.

'Nobody understands the mind of an Arab,' he said. 'God didn't mean us to, so we might as well stop trying. It's not just money with them, there's poetry comes into it, and real religion, and gentleness and ruthlessness, and wild rages, and love and generosity inside hard bargaining, and simplicity and cunning—and just to make it easier, there's Arabs and Arabs. I had time to do a lot of reading in hospital, after my accident.'

He touched the scar on his face.

'Jews don't understand Arabs,' he said harshly and suddenly. 'Arabs understand Jews, but Jews don't understand Arabs—otherwise there wouldn't be all this darned trouble. The Russians wouldn't be in Egypt in strength. If Jews had understood Arabs, the Russians wouldn't be there.'

I noted his tone and the use of the word Jews instead of Israelis, and guessed that Ben Cullon was anti-semitic.

As if he read my thoughts, he said:

'Mind you, I'm not anti-semitic, don't get me wrong.'

'I don't get you wrong,' I said, and meant it, though not in the way he hoped, and added, for the second time that evening: 'I don't see why the Israelis shouldn't have their little slip of territory. They waited two thousand years to go back to Palestine and Jerusalem. It was their dream.'

He leaned forward, said:

'Okay, then, next time you're in Rome, tell the Italians to come and take over Britain, they had some Roman legions there a couple of thousand years ago. Their descendants must be dreaming like hell of going back to Britain.'

'They wouldn't accept the offer, not with our weather they wouldn't,' I said lightly, but he wasn't listening, and he looked round as Marion Cullon came in and handed me an envelope, and said Alex Ford had just left it for me. I guessed it was from Ducane.

Alex had dropped it in for me. To be handed to me. Casually. Just like that. I reckoned it was typical of the casual way Frank Baker had been running the outfit.

I opened the outer envelope, and then the inner envelope, and read the signal from Ducane:

'Turkish replacement for Kadem arrives this evening. Name, Hasan Demirel. Cover story, business man. Staying Hotel Lysander, Kyrenia. Using British passport name R. Manning for greater security and ease of movement through Cypriot-Greek territory. Ref. Air-Athene disaster. Confirmed that Istanbul station reports Turks affecting to accept Kadem death as accident. Second assassination would be unacceptable as would attempt at it, repeat attempt at it. Cyprus government would be regarded as unable to maintain order, repeat unable to maintain order, and protect Turkish inhabitants. Demirel's stay short. Probably three or four days, to pick up threads, get to know personalities. Am not hopeful. Do your best—Ducane.'

At least Ducane's Turkish station seemed well informed. I read the signal again, feeling that something was missing, and handed it to Ben Cullon. He'd known about Kadem, he might as well know about Demirel. He read it and handed it back.

'That guy in London is certainly business-like.'

I knew then what was missing, and what Cullon meant. I nodded, but he'd turned his back. He said:

'I guess even the Russian KGB mob would have put in a word of regret about Frank if he'd been one of theirs.'

'You don't know Ducane,' I said. 'The sentiment's there, but he doesn't express it.'

'I'll say he doesn't!'

'I know Kenneth Ducane—you don't,' I retorted defensively.

'I guess you must be psychic to know that guy.'

I shook my head and said nothing, because it would have taken a long time to explain Ducane's complex character, and bade him goodnight. I'd only been in Cyprus twenty-four hours.

I am not psychic.

If I had been, I wouldn't have shown him Ducane's signal.

I rang for breakfast at eight o'clock. Later, sitting on my balcony in the sun, in my dressing gown, sipping coffee, life seemed temporarily tolerable, even though death was in the headlines of the paper they sent up, as it was bound to be. Front page stuff and screaming:

'CYPRUS AIRLINER EXPLODES
60 MILES FROM LAND
"Ball of Fire in Sky"

The Air-Athene airliner over-due at Athens since yesterday morning, on a flight from Nicosia, Cyprus, is now believed to have blown up about sixty miles from its destination.

Air-sea rescue services have reported oil and floating debris. The possibility of survivors is now considered remote, but the search is continuing.

Two fishermen in a small boat from an island near to the mainland heard the plane approaching at a high altitude. One of them said later:

"I looked up at it without much interest, since we often see planes. Suddenly I heard what sounded like an explosion and it seemed to glow like a ball of fire in the sky. I saw a cloud of smoke and bits and pieces of the plane falling away from it.

"Almost at once it hurtled down and struck the sea. I do not think anybody could have survived."

In addition to the crew of five there were twenty-two passengers, mostly Greek or Greek Cypriots, but among those missing is a British passenger, Mr Frank Baker, long resident in Cyprus, and Mr Mahmoud Kadem, a Turkish business man from Istanbul.

In addition to the air hostess there were five other women and two children on the aeroplane.

An Air-Athene official said last night: "This is the first disaster of its kind involving an Air-Athene plane. An enquiry into the possible cause will be held."

A lucky escape was that of a Mr W. A. Anderson, believed to be a British subject from London, who had booked a seat on the airliner but subsequently cancelled it.'

I put the newspaper down, thinking good old Anderson, whoever he was, lucky old him, he'd dine out for years on his escape, meanwhile Frank Baker was dead, and Mahmoud Kadem was dead, and there wasn't any doubt it seemed in Ducane's mind about the cause. He'd used the word assassination in his signal.

Crew, passengers, and owners were in the clear. But a bomb is a bomb is a bomb. It doesn't walk on to an airliner on little plastic legs of its own.

Bombs are coddled and cossetted, they're spoilt darlings, their every whim pandered to, they're carried gently around until, for each one, according to time, place, and circumstances, a comfortable little niche is found among the luggage or among the crates of food and drink, there to slumber, there to awake in fury and repay its master for his trouble.

Down below on the beach the newly arrived tourists were emerging, white bodies eager for the heat of the sun. Some resembled thin dry insects, a praying mantis or a stick insect, others looked like pallid soft maggots. The human body is brittle or squashy, totally defenceless in itself against external violence such as bombs.

I lit a cigarette, thinking, they won't try the same trick twice, that's for sure, they'll guess that Derimel's plane will be searched inch by inch before he leaves Cyprus, or he'll be switched to another plane at the last moment.

This time, if there was a this time, there could be no question of faking an air accident, or probably any other kind of accident. This time it would have to be an out and out assassination and to hell with the consequences. If he was only to stay a few days they would have to move fast.

A normal killing needs time to set up. Method and an escape route must be arranged, and money provided, because the normal modern assassin likes to have a chance of getting away. He's got no sense of humour. He's getting self-centred.

The old time assassins, who killed with bombs or bullets and were arrested at once—the ones who went to the wall with defiant revolutionary cries and a flamboyant gesture, they're in short supply, they're getting thin on the ground having been largely killed off. Times change, not necessarily for the better, and the cost of political murder, like the cost of living, goes up every day.

Looking down on the thin stick-insect bodies, and the plump maggot bodies, stumbling down the beach to swim and sit in the sun, I thought that a bomb in the Thessides Hotel would do them no good at all. It'd be a question of snap or squish. Aesthetically unattractive, most of them, mentally sluggish and conversationally dull, perhaps, but innocent and vulnerable. Not meriting a snap or squish. The same applied to the Hotel Lysander where Hasan Demirel was staying.

I was finishing dressing when the phone rang. I thought it might be Alex Ford surfacing, suggesting a meeting, but it was Damon Nicolaides.

His voice sounded shaky.

Remembering what Ahmet Aksu had said, I guessed it was love trouble. Woman palaver. And I felt bored. If his Turkish bint had been confined to her house in Famagusta, then that was too bad. He needn't think I was going to resue her. I had grave doubts about the whole Romeo and Juliet set-up, and thought Frank Baker foolish to get involved.

Cyprus might be the island of Aphrodite, Goddess of Love, but in the present circumstances young Greek godlings could not expect to fall in love with young Turkish maidens and get away with it, not unless Aphrodite had more influence than she seemed to have.

But he sounded so agitated that I clearly had to see him if only to turn down whatever request he had in mind, and we arranged to meet at 'the usual Kyrenia café', which wasn't a café at all but a group of trees about ten miles outside the town.

From what Frank had told me, Damon Nicolaides would catch the early morning convoy from Nicosia, sail through the Turkish zone under the aegis of the United Nations to Kyrenia, and then hitch-hike a lift.

Cumbersome, but reasonably secure.

Chapter Six

I was in a bad mood when I spotted him sitting under the carob trees, and stopped and drove off with him. He was pale and tight-lipped, and referred only briefly to the air-crash.

I felt my irritation mounting. It was not that I was unsympathetic to young lovers' dreams, it was just that I didn't want to be involved in tears and arguments and pleas for intervention, I had other things on my hands such as Demirel exposing himself to assassination in a hotel, and Ahmet Aksu in Nicosia, muttering about a new group of terrorists.

'Something happened last night,' began Damon at once, but I cut him short.

'Not now, in a minute.'

He lapsed into a sulky silence, lit a Greek cigarette, and said nothing more till I had turned off the road along a former cart-track which led to a headland and a view of the sea. I pulled the hand-brake on and switched off the engine.

'All right,' I asked, 'what's on your mind?'

Damon Nicolaides shrugged, opened his side window, and threw his cigarette-end out, and said nothing.

'What's on your mind?' I asked again.

'I do not want us to meet again, that is all.'

'As you wish. Suits me okay.'

It certainly did. I tried not to show my pleasure.

'You're not the only agent we've got,' I added. 'Or I should say not the only ex-agent we've got, seeing you are no longer on the pay-roll.'

It was a rough reply.

I don't know why I was so rude, except that he could have put things more tactfully. I assumed he didn't like me, had heard of Frank's death, and was going to make his own arrangements in future. So I was pleased—but piqued. I was also wrong.

'Last night I met a man called Spiros,' Damon Nicolaides muttered. 'He came up to me in a café. I do not know his other name. He said it was he who had arranged for me to be expelled from AKEL, even though he knew I was a good Communist.'

I switched sideways to look at him. He was staring straight

ahead. I said:

'He had you expelled even though he knew you were a good Communist? Why?'

'That's what I said to him, I said why? He said the Cypriot Communist Party was getting too bourgeois—too respectable—but was still watched by the Special Police. He didn't want me watched by the police. So he had me expelled, Mr Carter.'

'He didn't want you watched by the police? You are sure he said that?'

He nodded, massaging the forefinger of his left hand nervously.

'Go on,' I said, thoroughly alert now. But he continued to massage his finger. His face was taut and worried.

'Go on,' I said again. 'What happened then?'

Nicolaides licked his lips.

'He wanted me to join a group of activists.'

'What group?'

'That is what I said, "What group?" I said. He said it did not have a name. But if I wanted a name he would call it IN-AKEL, meaning INNER-AKEL, though it had nothing to do with AKEL. He said there would be only ten people in it, eight others, him, and me. He was a Marxist, I could tell from the words he used, "progressive", "imperialism", "demands", "peace loving", words like that.'

'Was he pro-Russian or pro-Maoist?'

He did not reply. Most Intelligence work is dull routine stuff. Now and again you get a chance of a breakthrough to something hot. I reckoned I was on the edge of one now.

I guessed that Damon had overplayed his part in the past. He'd been too revolutionary for the orthodox Cypriot Communist Party. But he'd become a prime target for others. Frank Baker had lost him as an AKEL agent. Dozing in the island sun, Frank hadn't realised that the Party had temporarily changed its tactics, was aiming at respectability. Yet now Frank's error, ironically, was bearing fruit.

Nicolaides was pushing the knuckles of his hands together now. He said, abruptly, but in almost a whisper:

'Sir, I wish to go now, please.'

I looked at him coldly.

'You telephone me, you meet me, and now suddenly you want to go after five minutes. This IN-AKEL thing, what did they want you to do, tell me that. I'll find out, don't kid yourself,' I bluffed, 'so you might as well save me time and trouble. Okay?'

The sun was hot but a slight sea-breeze kept the interior of the car cool. In the distance I could make out squat Kyrenia Castle, but a pocket of cloud obscured Fort Hilarion in the mountains where the vulture had floated past on deceptively peaceful honey-brown coloured wings. A cicada ticked loudly, in a patch of coarse grass and spring flowers to the right of the car, and I waited saying nothing. I might have guessed what his reply would be.

'There is a Turk here,' Nicolaides said at last, in a sad, hopeless voice.

'I know.'

'He is called Hasan Demirel. He arrived yesterday.'

'I know.'

'They want to kill him. They want me to kill him. The man who spoke to me said Turkey and Greece are tools of American imperialism. They do not want peace between Greek Cypriots and Turkish Cypriots, or between Greece and Turkey.'

He was speaking rapidly now, in a low monotone, the words tumbling over each other, as though he wanted to get them out before he again thought better of it.

'I am telling you this, Mr Carter, sir, for the same reason I worked for Mr Baker in AKEL, because I am a religious man, and Selin, she is religious in her own religion, and we respect each other's religions, and Communists don't, and also because you and Mr Baker have been kind to me and Selin and——'

'What did you answer,' I interrupted. 'Never mind the rest of it—tell me what you replied.'

You had to have luck in Intelligence, Ducane always said so, you ought to know how to exploit it when it turned up, but it was no good having know-how unless you had luck. With luck you might muddle through without know-how. But not vice versa.

I sat listening to the cicada in the grass, waiting for Damon Nicolaides to speak, knowing that if Damon had made the right reply this could be the break-through, the beginning of a trail which could lead to a vulture's nest.

'I told you I did not wish to do this work any more,' Nicolaides said in a dull voice.

I felt the optimism and high hope draining away from inside me.

'I told him I would not do it.'

Nicolaides fumbled at his Greek cigarettes in the blue and white pack.

'I said I had served the cause enough, and was going to America with my girl. I would not join this thing he called INAKEL.'

The cicada went on ticking in the grass. I offered him a light, struggling against my bitter disappointment. I noted that the cigarette was trembling in his lips as he bent towards the flame. Then he stared straight ahead, taking quick puffs, his lips quivering between the drags.

I was thinking that luck hadn't run out, it hadn't even begun.

Damon Nicolaides lowered his head and passed his left hand across his brow and then looked up, hot-eyed and angry, and said:

'I am a Greek, Greeks always talk too much. Why did I tell him I planned to go to America with my girl Selin, to marry her, to live there? When I said I had served the Marxist cause enough, he said, "We must go on serving all our life". I told him what I planned—but lightly, sir, as I could say, "Tomorrow we go to Paphos", or maybe, "Sunday we drive to the Troodos mountains to picnic"—no thought to what I was saying. Why did I say it?'

I looked at him, mystified, unable to foresee the pay-off, any more than Damon Nicolaides had foreseen it.

'Now I will tell you what happened, now you shall learn what happened, but then will you help me?'

I hesitated, then nodded, saying nothing, thinking, well, I've nothing to lose, maybe he's got something to lose, but I haven't, I'm starting with nothing and I can't end up with less.

'If I can, I will,' I said slowly.

'That much you promise?'

'If it's a question of money, I might have to refer the matter to——'

Nicolaides interrupted eagerly. His quick, volatile spirits seemed to have rocketed up from the depths into some sort of temporary sunshine.

'It is not a question of money, so you will help me, you promise?'

'If I can, I will,' I said again. 'Yes, I will.'

He sighed with relief, and flung his cigarette out of the window, though it was only half smoked.

'Now I am happy!' he said, and laughed.

'I'm not,' I said sourly.

Nicolaides swung round on the bucket seat, so that he faced me and put his arm along the back of the driver's seat.

'This man looked at me, sir—cold and thoughtful. He said, "Thank you for telling me that. I knew you had a Turkish girl called Selin, I did not know you were going to America, comrade. A strange choice." "I am in a strange position," I said, and felt uneasy because I did not like the look on his face. Then he smiled, and he said, "Comrade, if you wish to become an American citizen you will have a form to fill, and you will be asked if you have been a member of the Communist Party. Naturally you will write 'no', because Cyprus is a long way away. Nobody in AKEL would betray you, comrade." That's what he said, and now I felt easier, and nodded and smiled at him. He did not smile back, but I thought, well, some people smile often and some hardly at all.'

I thought he was loosening up, as Greeks will when they begin to tell a story. But he removed his arm from the back of the seat and fumbled in his blue and white pack for another cigarette. I looked at him, waiting for him to go on, noting that now some of the earlier tension had returned.

'Then he said, quite slowly, "None of our little activist group would tell anything to the American capitalists about a comrade who had *helped* us, as I am asking you to help. We'd keep quiet about a comrade like *that.*" Sir, it was blackmail, and I said, "But I have been expelled from the Party," and he said, "Yes, you have been expelled for having Maoist tendencies, comrade. You understand, of course?" And I did understand, because as you know, sir, Maoist Communists are even more left-wing than orthodox comrades. But I said, no, I would not help them to kill the Turk, because I do not like killing people, and he said, "Have you tried it, comrade? It is not difficult," and he smiled then, for the first time, not much, but a little, quickly.'

'So you said no again?'

'My heart was in despair, but I said no. He said he would be in the Delos Café this evening, if I changed my mind, just in case. But I said no.'

'A pity,' I said bleakly.

'I do not want to do this secret work any more.'

'You don't need to go on saying it.'

I spoke slowly, appalled at what I knew I should do, wondering if I could do it, remembering Ducane's signal about the Turks affecting to treat the death of Kadem as an accident, but it would be different if Demirel, too, were killed.

Damon Nicolaides said confidently:

'So I will write "no" on the form I must fill in, and you will tell the American government people that it is only a paper lie, because I joined AKEL to fight Communism and that I worked well.'

I was hardly listening, letting his words flow over me, imagining the sputter of rifle fire and the crash of bazookas, as the communal fighting broke out again, seeing once more the burnt-out villas in the Turkish suburb outside Nicosia, the bullet holes in the walls of the Turkish Club, smelling smoke, not spring flowers outside the car, hearing screams above the ticking of the cicada in the grass. I heard him say:

'I joined AKEL for Mr Baker, who was a good friend of my father, and Mr Baker promised always to help me.'

The tone was suddenly unsure, wheedling, almost pleading.

I did not look at him, I bent my head to light my pipe, to gain time, anchoring my thoughts to hard facts, such as two Turkish sea-borne landings from Anatolia, where there was already a sizeable concentration. Almost certainly there'd be two landings, one around industrial Limassol, and one around Famagusta relying for help on the big Turkish community there. And then a two-pronged advance inland on Nicosia, carefully by-passing the British Base at Dhekelia on the one side, and the Troodos Mountains on the other. And an air drop astride the Kyrenia–Nicosia road in the north, into friendly Turkish agricultural lands, linking with the Turkish garrison at St Hilarion, then an advance towards Nicosia.

So it would be a three-pronged attack, not two, from south, east, and north, I thought, waiting for my heart to harden.

'Mr Baker promised always to help me, as you have promised to help me,' I heard Nicolaides say. 'It will cost no money, so there will be no difficulty. Will there?'

'Sometimes these things are not as easy as they seem,' I temporised, struggling with the remnants of my conscience.

'This thing is easy,' I heard him whisper desperately. 'Costing no money, sir, just a letter or a message.'

I nodded, not in agreement with Nicolaides, but in agreement with the argument which was now beginning to build up inside me. Nicolaides misunderstood the nod, and smiled, but I ignored the smile, letting the argument build up, layer upon layer, telling me that handsome Romeo might in the end find another Juliet, and pretty Turkish Juliet, if put to it, might find another Romeo, but what of men and women and children, isolated by mobs, cut off when the storm broke, heads smashed by bullets and clubs? Where to find other heads? What consolation if Turkey and Greece went to war, the Security Council met, Britain stirred uneasily, the United States Sixth Fleet was moved from A to B and on to C and back to A?

Still no new heads, no new shattered bodies. Only blood and, in places, food for vultures.

'I'll help you,' I said. 'In the end, I will.'

Damon guessed my meaning.

'In the end?'

I nodded.

'That's what I said. You'll have to play along with this man called Spiros. Meet him this evening. Tell him you've thought it over, changed your mind. Then I'll help you.'

Nicolaides said nothing. He was staring straight ahead, again twisting the forefinger of his left hand with his right hand. He turned and looked at me, his face reflecting a mixture of pain and astonishment.

'You are playing Spiros's game.'

'I'm playing it better.'

'Blackmail—you, too?'

He was still unable to believe it.

'Call it business,' I said.

Nicolaides shook his head. He stopped massaging his finger. He seemed to have made up his mind.

'I shall have nothing more to do with Spiros.'

'It's your choice, kid.'

'We will go to America. And in due course I will apply for citizenship without your help,' he added bitterly.

I said nothing, my mind struggling for strength in the mire of bad faith, because if you are going to indulge in treachery you've got to do it properly, you've got to win.

No point in half measures, no point in being semi-treacherous and losing. I had another card to play, but the thought of it sickened me.

I stared into the driving mirror, watching the occasional lorry and car passing along the main road behind us, noting a brown Volkswagen which had drawn up by the roadside some distance away, and had been there since soon after I had arrived with Nicolaides. It was probably tourists admiring the view. I hoped it was tourists admiring the view.

Above the sound of the cicada I heard Nicolaides say:

'Perhaps Spiros will forget.'

I said nothing, letting him stew for a while, and started the engine and turned the car and rejoined the main road to Kyrenia passing the Volkswagen, which was empty, but that didn't mean much because there was undergrowth and a ragged lemon grove nearby.

Nicolaides, pursuing with volatile Greek optimism his new found vein of hope, said:

'You break your promise, all right, you break your promise, but I do not care, I think Spiros will forget, I do not think he will do anything, I do not think he will tell the American government people that I belonged to AKEL.'

I took a deep breath and said:

'Maybe not—but I will.'

For a moment he thought I had changed my mind, and a wonderfully happy look came over his face.

'I'll tell them you were a genuine Communist, and I'll deny you ever worked for me,' I said, plunging the dagger. 'Provided they even let you into the country,' I added, giving the dagger a twist. After a while I glanced sideways. His eyes were filled with tears.

We drove in silence and parted by the carob trees near Kyrenia, where I had picked him up, without speaking or a farewell nod.

I drove slowly off.

In the driving mirror I saw Nicolaides walking down the middle of the road, a small forlorn figure in the mid-day heat. Then I saw him break into a run and wave, and stopped and waited for him, engine running. It was what I expected.

He came to the driver's window, panting and flushed, and said:

'All right. It will be as you say. I'll tell Spiros I've changed my mind. I'm doing it for Selin, not you.'

He looked at me with hate in his eyes. I nodded and said:

'I will see you tomorrow at Rendezvous 3.'

He shrugged indifferently, and turned away, but as I revved up the engine and began to let in the clutch he turned back, and again put his head down to the driver's window.

'There used to be a story that an Englishman's word was as good as his bond. I expect the story was made up by an Englishman.'

The hatred in his eyes was now mingled with contempt, and the mixture was such that I believed that if he had had a gun he would have shot me. It was a thought which was to return.

'It depends on the value of the bond,' I muttered, and quickly drove off, trying to find some significant meaning in my words, and deciding there wasn't any. But I had to say something.

I went back to the Thessides Hotel, hating myself, hating my work for the first time. I had never before visualised breaking faith with an agent, never contemplated personal treachery and blackmail. Whether Spiros was or was not under outside control, whether he was The Vulture, or just a little falcon, a small merciless merlin with fierce yellow eyes, Damon Nicolaides had been right. I had played the same game as Spiros.

But I'd played better because I had used bluff.

Spiros, from vindictiveness, and as an example to others, might have had no hesitation in carrying out his threat. But I wouldn't have carried out mine. I would have told the Americans the truth, I'd have helped him in the end. If he'd held out he'd have won.

But he couldn't know that.

He'd wanted to opt out. He wanted a peaceful life now, love and family, and all that, and Cyprus, Island of the Goddess of Love, was the worst place to begin it in. He was the wrong guy in the wrong place at the wrong time.

Too bad, just too bad. I repeated the words aloud, too bad, just too bad, but it didn't help me kid myself along, I thought dismally, playing the hard-boiled type didn't help. Too bad for Damon! All that easy stuff. But you've got down to Russian KGB level. You've touched pitch. Whatever the motive, you've touched the black stuff. Things won't be the same again, maybe nearly the same, but not quite the same.

Then suddenly I felt furious at the injustice of it all. Settle for ethics, for personal loyalty, for the Englishman's bloody word, and his stinking damned bond, and you risk slaughter in the island. Touch pitch to try to avoid it, and there's a black cloud of conscience hanging over you no bigger than the United States of America.

Again I wished I'd never come to Cyprus. I went further. I thought it would be nice to be a hermit in a hole in the ground, living off honey and wild locusts, and scratching and grunting.

I parked the car in the front of the hotel and walked round to the back where there was an open-air bar overlooking the sea and the swimming pool, and chairs and tables and bright umbrellas. I went to the bar and ordered an *ouzo*. Ben Cullon was taking a pre-lunch swim. I watched him, blond, lean and sun-tanned, run along the diving board and do a header into the pool. At a nearby table a middle-aged woman said to her husband:

'I didn't think the breakfast was at all good.'

Her husband went on reading the *Cyprus Mail*. She gave the matter further thought and added: 'No, I didn't. I didn't think it was at all good. And they charge too much for the extra orange juice. Much too much.'

I swallowed the *ouzo* and ordered another, thinking of communal rioting and the hermit life, and vultures, but on her own level she was right. They did charge too much for the orange juice. And it's all very well to sneer, but you can only judge things with your own yardstick. For the old English faggot orange juice was important. She was right to mutter about it.

I watched Ben Cullon haul himself out of the swimming pool, and roughly towel himself down. He spotted me as he came back to the hotel and called out cheerfully:

'Hiya, fella!'

I waved to him. I would mention the price of orange juice some time. I could do it without causing offence. Ben was a good bloke, I was glad to have him to talk to. It was all very well being a lone wolf, but only within reason. An agent could talk freely to his spymaster. but to whom could the spymaster talk? Where did the buck stop? On the need-to know principle I could talk with Ben about some things. But not everything.

Still, better than nothing.

I finished the drink and walked slowly into the hotel for a wash before lunch, toying with the thought of confiding in Ben about the Nicolaides affair, deciding that I couldn't. Burdens of conscience add up to a lump which should remain in your own pocket.

Marion Cullon was talking to a receptionist behind the desk near the main entrance. Her dark French-Canadian hair and olive complexion contrasted pleasantly with the aquamarine dress she was wearing. They were a good couple, well-suited, extroverts, and still in love. In a world of arid hatred and intrigue Ben and Marion Cullon were a clean, refreshing oasis.

I went up to her, and murmured:

'Somebody's complaining about the price of the breakfast orange juice!'

She smiled happily.

'I told Ben he was charging too much! Thanks.' She looked triumphant. 'There's a letter for you,' she added, and reached up to the pigeon holes behind her.

I took it and walked into the dining-room, turning it over in my hand, noting the lack of a postage stamp and that it was written on Palaestra Hotel paper, Kyrenia. I knew of nobody at the Palaestra Hotel, The handwriting was large and feminine. I opened it. It read:

'Dear Mr Carter,

I arrived today and am staying here for a few days reliving some old memories, and wonder if you would care to have coffee and brandy with me this evening. I would appreciate it if you kept the contents of this letter to yourself for reasons which will be apparent when we meet. I know of a mutual friend in London.

Yours sincerely,
Hellena Christiansen.'

I spent the afternoon lazing on the terrace, thinking about Damon Nicolaides and speculating about Hellena Christiansen. Hellena was a Greek name. I guessed she was Frank's girlfriend in Athens, and wondered why she wanted to keep the meeting confidential. I could understand a masochistic wish to indulge in a nostalgic visit to the island. But I saw no reason for the secrecy.

After a while I grew tired of thinking and went to sleep.

At tea-time Ben Cullon came out carrying some new colour photographs he had developed and printed during the afternoon. One was of nearby Bellapais Abbey, honey hued against a blue sky and sea, contrasting with another which showed Kykko Abbe, dark against a storm gathering in the Troodos mountains. Simply framed, they would be on sale to tourists soon at thirty shillings each.

Not much of a profit, but Ben's obvious energy had to have its various outlets, and Ben was clearly not one to pass up the odd dollar, whether on orange juice or colour shots. Everything had to show a profit.

I envied Ben Cullon his peaceful straightforward existence, his prosperous hotel, his pretty wife, and his healthy extrovert attitude to life. I didn't begrudge him these things. He was a nice guy. It was a pity that he was anti-semitic. But then if he hadn't been, he would not have become friendly with Saleh Karim, the Arab, and introduced Karim to Frank Baker, for what it was worth, which didn't seem much. Saleh Karim, with his murky trade in passports, wasn't much use, as far as I could see. I thought Frank must have been scraping the bottom of the barrel to take him on at all.

After tea I strolled along the coast to Alex Ford's house and asked him to check Hellena Christiansen's name in a signal to London. I found him at work with secateurs among the roses, in an open necked shirt, showing a scrawny neck, sun-tanned and relaxed. I had thought there might even be a message from London about Hellena Christiansen. But there wasn't one. I had a drink with Alex Ford, gentle and benevolent; he went on a bit about the Ninth Roman Legion, which had been stationed in Britain and then completely disappeared and nobody knew why. It didn't seem to me to matter much, taking the sweep of history as a whole. I returned to the Thessides Hotel, envying him his neat house and garden, his probable friendships among the English colony in Cyprus, his whole uncomplicated existence. All he had to do was to be on hand with his receiver-transmitter, twice a day, for a few minutes, and he'd earned his salary. It was money for old rope.

I was envying everybody that evening.

The sun was setting against distant black headlands as I strolled back. It was all deceptively peaceful. I didn't think it would last, and was still depressed by what I had done to Damon Nicolaides.

Frank Baker would not have done it. Certainly not Alex Ford. Perhaps I should have offered him an outright bribe of a very large sum. But I had no authority. And time was too short. So what I had done, I had done.

One had to sweat it out.

Chapter Seven

There was no difficulty in identifying Hellena Christiansen. She was sitting alone on the terrace of the hotel. The rest of the tourists were inside looking at a display of Greek folk-dancing.

After a slight formal hesitation I introduced myself and sat down and she poured out a cup of coffee. It was difficult to see her clearly in the subdued lighting. But she had an oval face, and a straight nose, her hair seemed to be bronze and thick, shaped short, round her head, and her eyes light rather than dark, though whether they were grey or blue I could not tell.

She seemed of medium build, perhaps in her early thirties, though you can't tell these days, even in daylight, and her arms and legs, wrists and ankles, were slim. Her shoulders sloped classically from her neck, and she wore two gold bangles and two pearl ear-rings. Her voice was modulated and pleasant, and she had a slight, indefinable foreign intonation, and that was about all I took in at first.

I hadn't known what to expect, and suddenly realised I didn't even known the name of Baker's girl in Athens. It was all assumption. Perhaps I had jumped to the wrong conclusions. Maybe she was another girl-friend. From Rhodes, or Crete, or Naples, or Corfu, or Istanbul. Men on their own in my mob, and in the Eastern Mediterranean, can lead widely esoteric lives.

'When did you arrive from Athens?' I asked politely.

It was a shot in the dark and she recognised it as such.

'How do you know I arrived from Athens?'

'Just a guess. I knew Frank had a friend in Athens. They didn't tell me her name in London. I suppose they didn't think we'd meet. So it was just a guess,' I repeated, and made the usual noises about the air crash, waiting resignedly for the trembling of the lips and the flood of tears, because if this was a nostalgic visit, as she had written, I reckoned she'd start as she meant to go on.

I sat back fastening my emotional safety-belt.

I needn't have worried. Like Ben Cullon's, her remarks were regretful but cool. I was puzzled more than shocked, because it was difficult to link this attitude to a nostalgic visit. She gave me a thoughtful look and said:

'I flew over last night.'

'What time did you land?'

'About ten forty-five. We were a bit late. Brandy?'

'Thank you.'

I offered her a cigarette and she in turn said thank you. I thought, brandy, cigarette, thank you, thank you—fencing around, watching each other covertly, getting the feel of each other's personality; she, sitting upright, yellow dress against the dark blue canvas of the terrace chair, oval face calm but alert; bare brown arms and shoulders; poised, slow movement of the hand carrying cigarette to lips, and back to rest on the chair arm. And behind her a quick flashback of myself walking away from Alex Ford's house with a question at the back of my mind. Abruptly I asked:

'How did you know my name and where to find me, Miss Christiansen?'

'Mrs Christiansen, to be accurate. I don't wear a ring. I married a Norwegian stationed in Athens. We split up.'

We were sitting at right angles at the table. I turned my head to her and said again:

'How did you know my name, and where to find me?'

'I telephoned yesterday afternoon for the information. Do you mind?'

'I would have thought I'd have had a signal from London about you,' I said slowly. 'I'd have thought I'd have had a message saying you had enquired about me, and might come and meet me. I wouldn't have thought they'd have given my name and whereabouts to somebody without letting me know, that's not like London, that isn't, not like them at all. I checked this evening but there was no message from London about you—or about anything else, come to that.'

She smiled and said:

'A dull post. Perhaps you'll be lucky tomorrow, Mr Carter, that's the thing about the post, there's always the hope that tomorrow may——'

But I wasn't going to let her get away with it.

'So how did you know my name, Mrs Christiansen?'

She leaned forward and took a sip of coffee, then sat back, not smiling now.

'Are you interrogating me?'

'If I were, you'd know the difference.'

I was getting impatient, fed up with all this mysterious, withdrawn stuff. She was all right to look at, but she was a pain in the neck with all this fiddling about. 'You didn't hear from London because I didn't telephone London—and I didn't telephone Mr Ducane because I didn't know his number. Now are you happy?'

'I'm happier, but I'm not hopping up and down with joy, not yet, I'm not. Who did you telephone, then, and why the hurry?'

'Does it matter?'

'In my job it does.'

'So you *are* interrogating me?'

'Not yet, I'm not. But I'm edging up to it.'

'I don't like being interrogated, you know. What happens if I get up and walk away?'

Dear God, I thought, she's off again, yawing and flapping around. I said:

'Nothing happens if you walk away, *you* wanted to see *me*—not vice versa.'

She sighed and took a mouthful of brandy.

'I telephoned Saleh Karim.'

'Karim? I saw him last night—why didn't he tell me?'

'I asked him not to tell you—or anybody else.'

'He should have told me. I pay him. He should tell me everything I ought to know.'

'It depends what you ought to know.'

She was no longer leaning against the back of her chair. She was leaning towards me, her oval face earnest in the subdued lighting. I said brusquely:

'You're being difficult and evasive, Mrs Christiansen, I think you know what I mean—he ought to tell me everything involving me, for a start, that's for certain.'

'Not always. Not this time. You might have spoken about it to your friends. It would have been natural.'

'Not to me, it wouldn't, anyway I haven't got any friends, not here, except perhaps Ben Cullon and his wife and Alex Ford.'

She nodded.

'That makes three.'

I sat back in my chair and fumbled for my pipe. She was beginning to irritate me again. She was so enigmatic she might just as well have said nothing.

'Anyway, why shouldn't I speak about you and your arrival?'

'For a personal reason. You could call it a very personal reason. I wanted to be sure I'd arrive here. And I also wanted to make sure that if I arrived here I'd arrive alive. I could add that if I arrived alive, I wanted you to be alive, too. Otherwise the journey would have been expensive and pointless,' she added dryly.

The feeling of boredom and impatience increased in me. She was good looking enough not to need to pull the dramatic stuff in order to make herself interesting. It was either that, or she was a nut case. I half expected her to tell me in confidence that she had a wireless set in her head.

Casually, without thinking, I said, like a fool:

'Nothing much could happen to you on the hop from Athens.'

'Perhaps that's the sort of thing Frank thought. I'm surprised you say that.'

'That was a tragic accident.'

'It was sabotage,' she said softly.

She was staring around into the near distance where the terrace lighting merged into the shadows of trees and shrubs, eyes troubled.

'Can we go somewhere else? I don't think this is a good place to talk.'

There was rhythmic music inside the hotel, and lights and occasional applause. But the terrace was deserted except for ourselves, a wide expanse of chairs and tables, unoccupied except for our own table.

'What are you afraid of?'

'Being here. Pinpointed in light. Everybody inside except us. Let's go somewhere else. Please!'

She got up quickly, and led the way to the side of the terrace where some steps led down to the boulder-strewn sandy beach. I followed her until we were out of sight and earshot of anybody who might come out on to the terrace. We sat down in the shadow of a rock. She lit another cigarette and said:

'Your work, Frank's work, is a lonely business.'

I thought of the way I had had to treat Nicolaides and agreed. I wasn't surprised that Frank had told her the nature of his job. He was intending to marry her. It was fair that she should know.

'He discussed things fully with me.'

That did surprise me. I made no comment.

'Was that wrong?'

'It was his decision,' I said carefully.

'He was a very worried man. There were things he thought he could talk over with me which he could not report to his head office. Intangible things, sometimes, which would look foolish on paper. There was one thing in particular. He told me about it a month before he died. I shall never forget the anxious look on his face. And when he had told me I think he almost regretted doing so.'

'I think you had better let me know what it was, don't you?'

'I intend to. It will explain why I wanted you to keep our meeting a secret, why I told Saleh Karim not to mention it to you. You would probably have mentioned it to Frank's good friends Ben and Marion Cullon. Why not?'

'Why not?' I agreed, suddenly tense. 'I would probably have done so—why not?'

She stared out to where the black coast jutted into the moonlit sea.

'Frank thought he had possibly made a mistake about Ben Cullon—that's why not. He trusted even Saleh Karim more than the Cullons, and gave me Karim's telephone number.'

I felt the tension increasing inside me until it became a dull pain. I leaned forward and picked up a handful of pebbles, and threw one at a large white stone gleaming in the moonlight, and missed, and threw another, and then two more in rapid succession. Finally I threw the rest of them together, and swung round and stared at Hellena Christiansen's profile.

'What sort of mistake?'

She answered in the tight, controlled way people speak when they are about to lose control.

'He thought he had picked the wrong man as a confidant—that was his worry, that was one thought which must have been nagging at his mind when he went on that last flight. Not just worry about Kadem's safety—worry about this other thing. He dropped me a line a few days before he was killed. Up to then he'd said I could always get in touch with Cullon, if I wanted to. Now he said I wasn't to, and gave me Saleh Karim's telephone number.'

I thought it was a pretty lousy second choice, but kept quiet.

'He said he had found out "something rather disturbing

about our friend" which he would tell me about. That was the exact phrase he used, "something rather disturbing". Now we shall never know what it was.'

'Ben Cullon has co-operated all the time,' I said, speaking slowly, keeping it cool, thinking she was het up enough already; thinking, I don't want any bloody hysteria, that's the last thing I want, hysteria.

'Ben Cullon co-operated all the time before Kadem left for Athens,' I insisted.

'And look what happened when Kadem left for Athens. Look what happened to him. Look what happened to Frank, come to that.'

She had clasped her arms around her knees and was rocking backwards and forwards. Her voice was now deceptively flat. I knew it didn't reflect her feelings. I had heard that tone. Slightly higher pitched than usual, but flat, dead flat, indicating the moment before the breakdown. I couldn't do with a breakdown.

'Hellena?'

She stopped rocking and looked round at me. I have noticed on other occasions how the sudden unexpected use of a Christian name can have a steadying effect.

'Hellena, are you suggesting that Ben Cullon had a hand in the plane disaster?'

'I don't know. How should I know?'

'Tell me what Frank Baker would have told me. That's not asking much.'

She hesitated again, and I knew she was near the jump, and I heard Ducane talking, about a hundred years ago, with a wide grin across his frog-like face, and I heard Ducane say, 'There comes a point when they make the jump—and the jump is between what they want to say, what is the truth, and the residual doubts. You've got to keep the pressure up, Tom, but not too much, if you press too much they get kind of resentful and obstinate and dig their toes in.' So I paused and picked up some more pebbles. She did not wait for me to begin throwing them.

'Frank told me, the last time we were together, that he had been in Ben Cullon's office at Ben's invitation, having a drink before lunch, and Ben Cullon's desk was covered with papers, bills, and receipts and all the rest of it—and Ben Cullon was called out to speak to one of the people staying in the hotel. It was nothing important. Something about hiring a car. While he was away the phone rang. Frank answered it for him. It was some local shopkeeper querying an order. Frank took the message and scrabbled among the papers to find something to write it on. He found a blank sheet of paper.

'He also found Ben Cullon's Canadian passport. Inside the Canadian passport, protruding a little, was a British passport. It was as though the two——'

She groped for words.

'As though the two were regarded as one?'

She nodded. I sensed rather than saw that she had turned her head and was looking at me expectantly.

'Sure it wasn't one of the hotel guests' passports?' I asked, knowing it wasn't, leading her on, knowing that she realised that I was leading her on, smoothing the path for her.

'Not one of the hotel guest's passport. A passport originally destined for Beirut. On Saleh Karim's list which he gave Frank.'

It was an anti-climax. So one of Karim's passports was on Ben Cullon's desk. So why not? Ben Cullon, hotel proprietor, might well be mildly interested in the passports which Saleh Karim sold in Beirut. One might turn up among his guests.

'So?' I said indifferently.

'It was in the name of W. A. Anderson. Does that mean anything?'

I shook my head uncertainly, groping in my mind, because the name did ring a bell, very faintly, but the easiest thing was to shake my head. Then suddenly I saw myself reading the newspaper account of the air disaster, the fishermen, the explosion in the sky, the list of passengers, and the final winding up sentence. I said quickly:

'There was a W. A. Anderson booked for the flight to Athens when——'

She interrupted me.

'Frank glanced inside W. A. Anderson's passport. He was inquisitive by nature.'

'He was paid to be.'

'It said Anderson was born in York, England, in 1938, was five feet ten inches tall and had fair hair and blue eyes, and that was all right, nothing odd about that, Frank said, nothing odd about the passport at all, really—except that the passport photo was a photo of Ben Cullon, who goes in for photography, as you know.'

People make things up, I thought, they embroider stories, add bits and leave bits out, and they do it because they are afraid, or for material gain, or for vanity, but none of this applied to Hellena. She was not recounting her own exploit. She was telling a dead man's story.

I heard her firing a string of questions.

'Why did Cullon want a British passport? Why did he book a flight in another name? What was he going to do in Athens? Why didn't he mention his proposed visit to Frank, and say to his good friend Frank, "Fine, I'm going that way myself, we can fly over together." Didn't he want Frank to know? Did he suspect that Frank had found out something important about him? Was he going to fly out of Cyprus, where he might be recognised, flashing his Canadian passport, and land in Athens using the British one, and use the British one in Greece—or wherever else he was going? Why should he want to hide his identity? Why?'

I sat watching the play of the moonlight on the sea, listening to the questions pouring out of her, and knew she would come to the inevitable query.

'Why did he cancel his flight?' she ended, quieter now, calmed by her outburst.

'You're thinking what I'm thinking,' I said reluctantly. 'We might as well face it.'

From the hotel came a distant sound of dance music. The folk-dancers had gone. The folk themselves were going to dance. I plugged on:

'You're thinking Ben Cullon cancelled the flight because he knew there was going to be a bomb on the plane. You're thinking he let Frank go on the plane knowing he was going to his death, that's what you're thinking.'

She gazed at me with frightened eyes.

'That is just what I'm thinking, and I'm also thinking that if he knew I was seeing you so soon after Frank's death—he might wonder what I might tell you. That's why I tried to keep it a secret, Tom.'

In the loneliness of the beach the use of my Christian name seemed natural. But I hardly noticed it in the sudden threat which appeared. I said:

'You think Frank might have stumbled upon something big, or Ben Cullon thought he had, and Frank was in the way, or about to get in the way, about to put some big operation in jeopardy? Something big enough to justify the killing of innocent people and the loss of an air-liner. A slaughter of civilians, like you can get in a war, not small crook stuff, or even big crook stuff. National stuff.'

I got to my feet.

'We'd better meet again, I've got things to think about.'

She seemed reluctant to go back to the hotel.

'When?'

'Tomorrow. I'll pick you up at the hotel at twelve-thirty. Bring a swimsuit and a pack-lunch.'

She continued to sit on the ground, but I wanted to be gone, to be alone, to think things out, as I'd said. I put out my hand to help her to her feet, and we stood for a few moments looking at the sea.

I don't know what she was thinking, but I was thinking of Ben Cullon's car, which I had noticed near her hotel when I arrived. Not outside it, though there had been room to park it there, but fifty yards away, half off the road, in the deep shadows of some flowering shrubs.

It wasn't an elaborate measure to avoid being followed or observed. For that sort of thing he would have left the car much further away and better concealed. It was a sort of half-and-half measure, the automatic action of, say, an Intelligence officer who was not unduly worried about being observed, but on the whole would prefer not to be.

I didn't tell her about it. But I asked her how her letter had been delivered to me.

'I tipped one of the hotel people to bring it round by hand,' she said indifferently.

I said, ah yes, and nodded approvingly but I felt like saying, ho-hum and shaking my head. If our suspicions were right, she might just as well have laid the letter, open, on Cullon's desk. All my mail, incoming, or anything I posted in the hotel box, would be opened and scrutinised, and my telephone conversations recorded.

'Don't telephone me,' I said.

She looked round nervously at the group of black rocks nearby.

'I wish Frank hadn't confided in me,' she murmured bitterly. 'I hate the burden of secrets. I tried to discourage him, but he had to talk to somebody, I suppose.'

Gabby old Frank. I wouldn't have thought it of one of Ducane's mob.

We walked slowly back to where the steps in the cliff led up to the hotel. At my school we used to link arms when walking along the road from the House to the main buildings. It was a custom, and you did it even if you disliked the person with you. I still do it sometimes, automatically, and with some people it gives a wrong impression.

I did it now, and was surprised to feel her arm pressing my arm lightly to her side. But I've heard that danger and fear sometimes have unexpected aphrodisiac effects, and that what went on in the London air raid shelters in 1940 would have surprised the German bomber pilots—as though people were determined to have a last big bash before the last big bang.

At the foot of the steps leading up to the hotel I stopped and told her to go up alone, I would follow later. She hesitated, but I didn't explain. After a moment she probably guessed that the less we were seen together the better.

'Is there anything else I should do?'

'You might change your bedroom when you get back—if you can. Say you don't like the view—something.'

She thought this over and said she would try, and went up the steps towards the light and the music.

After a while I followed and left the hotel. Ben Cullon's Fiat car was gone, and I returned to my own hotel.

Chapter Eight

That was how it started. That was how I met her.

I lay on my side in the sand, looking at the remains of the picnic lunch, and at Hellena Christiansen, the beautiful animal, satisfied and sleeping in the warmth of the afternoon air.

Her feet and ankles and part of her legs had been in the sun for some time and I lightly placed a towel over them to prevent sunburn. She opened her eyes and smiled sleepily.

I bent over and kissed her, a light, cool kiss.

I did it because she was beautiful, and I like beautiful things, especially in swimsuits. She responded in the same cool way, and said again:

'I'm not falling in love with you.'

I replied as I had done before: 'Suits me all right,' and lay back again, fully awake now.

It did suit me, too. I didn't know what to make of her. It is always difficult to believe that a lovely creature can be cruel and ruthless. Dicky birds caught by cats know differently when it's too late, but I'm no dicky bird.

I began to peel another layer off the memory onion, looking at the small strip of plaster on the outside edge of my left hand. I'd told her I'd cut it that morning by leaning on a piece of sharp broken glass in the sand near my hotel, but it wasn't that way at all.

What had happened between my first meeting with Hellena Christiansen and our torrid picnic next day was odd in an alarming way.

When I left her I had gone back to the Thessides hotel and had a nightcap in the bar. Alex Ford came in looking dapper and clean in a beige suit, he always changed from open necked shirt and slacks into something a little formal in the evening, because you've got to keep up an appearance in front of the natives.

He had had a signal from London but hadn't brought it along because it was so simple. Nobody had heard of Hellena Christiansen in London. Full stop. End message.

We had a desultory conversation, in the course of which he

talked and I grunted. He had temporarily scrambled down from Hadrian's Wall and was pattering about among the Roman mosaic floors at Bignor, comparing them to their advantage with what he called the over publicised Roman discoveries nearer Chichester.

You can't abruptly leave a little red-faced retired major stranded among mosaic floors and dash for the exit, but I went up to my room as soon as I decently could, and brooded over what Hellena Christiansen had said, and the fact that London did not know of her.

I did not trust her, but as yet I could evolve no theory why I shouldn't. The fact that London did not know of her was not in itself sinister. Frank did not need to tell them all about his Athens girl-friend, but I would have thought he would have formally checked her name, and the check would be on record. But then Ducane had said Frank was in need of a long rest.

He had it now.

Uppermost in my mind was the startling suggestion that the outward frankness and honesty of Ben Cullon concealed another and darker personality, which had let Frank go to his death.

Lying on the top of the bed, for it was still warm, staring at the ceiling and then at the sky framed by the open balcony window, I recalled the sudden tension in me which had followed her words. But now, in the quiet of the night, away from the low confidential sound of her voice, her physical attraction, and her nervousness, real or simulated, I began to take another long, hard look at her.

I realised that all I had to go upon was her word.

I had no other evidence that Frank had spoken freely to her, or discussed his worries with her, or written her a letter saying that he had come upon something disturbing, or even that Frank had ever seen a passport in Cullon's possession in the name of W. A. Anderson. Whether he had such a passport could be checked with Saleh Karim, but there again the fact that Cullon had it did not prove that Frank had seen it.

She certainly knew of Karim, and of Ducane's existence. But had she learnt of them through Frank Baker—or had she been provided with the information by somebody else to make her story credible to me?

Was she, in fact, Frank Baker's girl from Athens, and if not what were her motives in contacting me?

If she wasn't, I thought I could guess the answer.

It was twisted and devious, like so much in the Intelligence world, where something that seems real often is not, and where unreality in the end proves to be fact, and you think that all is solved, only to find that a proven fact has itself been planted for an ulterior reason in accordance with a tortuous plan.

It is well known that Russian KGB officers take an intensive course in chess playing.

Now, therefore, staring alternately at the ceiling and the sky beyond the balcony, I came to the conclusion that Hellena Christiansen, she of the frightened demeanour, might not have been frightened at all and that the black insinuations against Ben Cullon might have been made for a purpose.

If this were true, then Hellena Christiansen was a disruption agent, deployed against me to sever my association with Ben, who had undoubtedly been of service to Frank, and could be to me and anybody who succeeded us. Perhaps somebody had said, 'Frank Baker's only got a crummy little network, but it's on to something. We don't like it. Bust it up.' For it was a fact that all Frank's agents had been recruited, directly or indirectly, through Ben Cullon, including even Alex Ford and his Roman mosaics. Frank had told me that on the way to the airport.

If Ben were suspect, they all were. You can bust up an outfit by sowing mutual suspicion, so that it just disintegrates, or you can kill and frighten people. Or you can combine both methods, to be on the safe side.

I should have fallen asleep but I didn't.

It was just as well. If I had done, I'd never have regained consciousness, except possibly for a few seconds of bemused terror and pain, as I gasped for air. Maybe not even that long.

As it was, I lay for an hour or so watching the ceiling and the sky, thinking of Hellena, and after a while I began thinking of her golden skin against the yellow dress, shoulders and arms and neck, and well moulded figure, and straight nose and wavy bronze-red hair.

Then it happened.

One moment there was the sky and the outline of trees and the rectangles of the balcony woodwork, and I had closed my eyes for a few seconds.

When I opened them again, I stared first at the ceiling and

then at the long French windows, open to let in the cool night air. Something was now obstructing the view of the sky and the outline of the trees.

A passing cloud had covered the moon so that the white woodwork showed less distinctly, but the outlines were still discernible, except for a central portion which was now hidden by something which had not been there before.

I felt a slight tingling of the hairs of my skin and lay perfectly still, staring fixedly at whatever it was, or might be, on the balcony, for I was still not sure whether or not my eyes were deceiving me.

The cloud completed its passage across the moon, and when the scene lightened I saw the man move quickly out of the moonlight from the balcony rails to the area of shadow around the French windows. He was wearing narrow dark trousers and a dark shirt, and, I suppose, rubber soled shoes, for he made no noise.

He paused for a whole minute on the threshold of the room, standing motionless, staring into the room, head and shoulders bent forward as though listening. He had something in his right hand which was too big for an automatic, but might have been a revolver with an extension such as a silencer.

So long as he was at a distance the advantage was his. I wanted to lure him closer, and breathed more deeply, so that he could hear it, and once gave a little snort as a sleeper sometimes will, and stirred slightly.

I saw him duck down out of my line of vision, so that he must have been crouching on his haunches. The bed creaked as I moved, and I took advantage of the noise to edge over towards the right side of the bed, still lying on my back, but now on the edge of it, and began the loud breathing again, and saw the pale blob of his face and his shoulders come into view as he straightened himself up. The outlines became bigger and darker as he cautiously moved into the room.

My clothes lay on a chair near the table, and my wallet and the contents of my pockets were on the table itself. I thought he might go towards them because it is always wise to assume a normal explanation until it is disproved.

But he by-passed them, so he either wanted to get at me before he ransacked the room at his leisure, or else he just wanted to get at me.

He was moving very slowly now, as though testing each step

for floor-board creaks. I watched him through eyes three-quarters closed, and hoped like hell that he would approach the right side of the bed, since I had to lure him close, and I thought he might, because there was a night table the other side, and he did.

I can't say I felt afraid, because once you are launched into action you don't, you're too occupied, but of course I was as tense as a coiled spring, which in fact was what I hoped I was. I was lying on my back with my left knee raised, pressing on the bed with my left foot and with my left hand.

I could see now that what he held in his right hand was not a pistol with a silencer, but a blackjack, and looped over his forearm was a short length of what looked like rope.

The old routine against attack with knife or blackjack is simple enough, and is both defensive and offensive, first to ward off the blow and then to disarm the attacker.

The first obvious movement is to ward off the blow, which is done by raising your left arm, elbow bent, and launching yourself against your foe, so that your left fore-arm comes horizontally against his raised arm and weapon. At the same time your right arm is flung behind his fore-arm and wrist, and your right hand locks on to your own left wrist.

The impetus of the attack and the weight of your body bears him back and topples him, while the leverage and pain which you bring to bear against his fore-arm and wrist is such that he drops the weapon, and you end up on the floor beside him. The rest is a normal rough and tumble.

It is certainly not difficult from a standing position, but I'd never tried it from a prone position.

I waited until he was a few feet away. He was semi-crouching now, left arm extended, left hand empty, positioned to press over my mouth in case he muffed his first blow and I tried to yell.

The hand holding the blackjack was only at waist level, which didn't suit me, but I reckoned he would raise it above shoulder level when I moved, and would try a wild swipe.

When he was about four feet away I pushed down with left foot and hand, switched sideways, and jumped him. In the brief moment before I was at him he reacted as I thought. Up came the blackjack, his hand level with his head. He hesitated a second or two to decide how he could connect with my head, and so he never started the swipe before I had the lock on him.

I completed the matter with the normal thigh throw, right thigh behind his right thigh, and down we went.

I tried to do a pivoting left leg lock, in which you swing your left leg across his throat. You end up with your body at right angles to his, his right arm between your legs, levering it against your right leg.

If necessary you can break his arm.

You can lie in this position indefinitely and have a quiet talk. If he doesn't want to come clean you can put increasing pressure on his arm. Very few people like to have their arm slowly broken, so a chat like this can be useful.

But it was silly to try it, because I wasn't properly positioned and bungled it. He freed his arm and wrenched clear and was up in a flash, and ran to the window and scrambled over the balcony rail, and dropped to a roof below, built over the hotel bar.

I heard him scrabbling down a sturdy vine up which he had doubtless come in the first place. Then there was silence.

I made no attempt to follow him. There was no knowing what other weapons he might have about him and in the dark he would have the advantage of me.

When I switched on the light I saw the blackjack which he had let drop on the floor by the bed, and near it what I had thought to be a length of rope. But it wasn't rope, it was a short length of sturdy four-strand wire, the end fashioned into a running noose, very handy for garroting.

It made me thoughtful. My left hand was bleeding slightly from a scratch made by a faulty broken strand of the wire which had lacerated me.

The obvious idea occurred to me that the man might have been Damon Nicolaides, who had motive enough. But Damon was thin, this man was thick-set.

I remembered a hard, sudden pain—not the laceration of wire—which had hurt me as I grappled with his left hand, finger pressed against finger.

It was a long shot. Many people wear rings on their third fingers, many people are stocky, and there are many Greek Cypriots. But Damon Nicolaides had mentioned the name Spiros. And Frank Baker had pointed out a stocky man, with a ring, whose name was Spiros.

After a glass of brandy and water and a cigarette I went to bed again, not bothering to shut the window. He wouldn't try the same trick twice.

Oddly, the memory of the assassination attempt didn't keep me awake long. Either you succeed or you fail, you win or you lose, and what's past is past, but I saw I might have to be more careful in future, and thought of my car.

The one thing which always worried me was the thought that somebody might put a bomb in the car. I don't know how to play that one. You open the door and the bomb goes off; or you open the door safely and sit in the driving seat and switch on the ignition, and the bomb goes off and you're a goner. You can't win.

At first, the attempt seemed to confirm in a measure the situation outlined by Hellena Christiansen. Ben Cullon had been at the Palaestra Hotel. I had seen his car. If Hellena and I had been observed having our long talk on the beach, then as the recipient of her information I was an obvious and urgent target.

He could deal with Hellena later.

I was Frank Baker's successor, and though Cullon might know a great deal he couldn't know how much Frank had discovered; neither could I now; neither could Hellena.

I began to think there must have been a good deal stored in Frank's mind when he went on that plane. Maybe one or two solid facts and a ragbag of bits and pieces, nuances and tentative deductions, which needed long and careful discussion with me on his return.

There had been so many other things about which to brief me prior to his unexpectedly sudden departure.

If Hellena was right, and a woman of integrity, and on our side, Cullon not only let him go to his death but watched him do so with a marked sense of relief. But was she on the level?

Now the curse of all Secret Service work began its insidious delving and tunnelling. The KGB are not the only ones who play chess.

Before I fell asleep, I imagined some grey-faced man in Moscow or Istanbul, or Athens, or even London, saying: 'Baker is gone. Weeds continually cut down grow discouraged. We will now liquidate Carter. In case we fail, we will put the woman Christiansen in touch with him. She will disrupt. She will sow suspicion about the man Cullon, and, as a result, about the agents introduced by Cullon. Thus the station will fall apart and must be built anew. This will take a long time.'

Then there was some cheap second-degree Walter Mitty stuff—them talking about me, Tom Carter, being an experienced operator and how they had to be careful of me.

And so to sleep.

The following morning, after a late breakfast, I decided to slip into the little town to buy a few toilet things before going to meet Hellena. I had parked the car the night before along the side of the hotel, under some trees, secluded on its own because the parking area in front had been crowded, and it was easier along the side.

I regretted that now, and walked round it slowly for a full two minutes, staring at it, not knowing what I was looking for, while the old bomb fear niggled at me. What could be put into an aeroplane could be put even more easily into a car parked overnight in a secluded place.

But I knew the longer I waited the bigger the fear would grow. I gave another hopeless look inside the car. Maybe I expected to see a wire leading from the courtesy light to something under the seat. Yet I knew it wouldn't be as obvious as that. In the end, I stopped thinking and abruptly unlocked the door and got in.

I had the same jab of fear as I switched on the ignition, and another when I heard the starter-motor turn over, and a minor one as the engine fired. All rather silly. Better to go with a bang than a whimper. One tells oneself that, but it doesn't help much.

I bought some razor-blades and toothpaste, and a newspaper, wondering whether anything of the Greek–Turk negotiations had leaked out yet, but there was nothing, and I returned to the hotel and collected my packed lunch and a bottle of wine, and a swimsuit and towel, and sat in the sun for an hour till it was time to pick up Hellena Christiansen.

Chapter Nine

So there we were, lying on the beach, after that first picnic.

You could say that a good deal had happened, one way and another, during the eighteen hours since I had met her, and I was still unsure whether she was a friend or an enemy.

Suddenly she said:

'I wonder what Frank knew.'

I thought it a damned silly remark, and ignored it, and said his death must have been heart-breaking for her, though privately I thought she was getting over it with astounding rapidity.

'It was very, very sad,' she said.

I looked at her and said: 'Very sad? Is that all? I thought you were going to marry.'

'So did he. So did I, at one time. It's a long story.'

'Condense it,' I said. 'Make it snappy, like you would for a news-flash on the radio.'

'He cropped up at the right time. Lots to talk about, two past lives to discuss. But no sense of humour—bad news. Boring in the end. But I was fond of him.'

'Big deal. And the other one, your ex-husband?'

'Same thing. Prospect of long Norwegian winters, with a sense of humour—that's bearable. Long winters with no humour—bad news. Not on.'

She was half asleep now.

'You seem accident prone,' I muttered.

'I'm glad Frank didn't know.'

'He knows now all right,' I said, and closed my eyes.

After a pause, when I thought she was asleep, she sighed and said:

'What about Ben Cullon?'

'What about him?'

'Just—what about him, that's all.'

I didn't say anything, only grunted quietly to show I'd heard her.

She said:

'Why is Cullon so friendly with Saleh Karim? Saleh is fat, ponderous, devious. Cullon is athletic, a Canadian, open and uninhibited. I've met Karim personally.'

I looked at her. Just how indiscreet had Frank been? I said: 'Saleh Karim doesn't like Israelis. Why should he? And Ben Cullon is anti-semitic. It's something in common, I've spent some time listening to Ben Cullon ranting about Jews, Zionism, the State of Israel, the Palestinians, the lot. It's like a disease, like leprosy in the old days. Once you've got it you can't do anything about it, it gets worse, it eats you away. They can cope with leprosy now, but not anti-semitism, not really, not when it's got a hold. The Russians were anti-semitic under Tsardom, they still are, whatever they say. So are the Poles. Ben Cullon caught the disease, that's all.'

She looked away and said almost to herself:

'From whom—the Russians? Or the Canadians? Or both? Frank told me the story of the Krogers.'

Maybe someone else had told her the story of the Russians who had come from Canada with Canadian passports to spy in England. Maybe she knew it anyway. But the Russians wouldn't try the same thing again. Or would they, since Cyprus was so far from England?

I said coldly: 'Hellena, why are you trying to put me off Ben Cullon?'

She looked round at me, her big eyes wide and seemingly surprised.

'Tom, I've told you—why are you *trying to defend him?'*

I did not answer. I said:

'This picnic nearly didn't take place.'

'Why? Work?'

'Not work. Death. Somebody tried to kill me last night. I lay awake thinking of what you'd said. Then I lay awake thinking I wanted to make love to you. So you could say that you saved my life. If you'd been ugly I wouldn't have stayed awake, and would have died. But you aren't, you're beautiful, so I didn't go to sleep, and lived. So you might as well go on being beautiful.'

Thus I spoke her fair words, and told her what had happened. But I still didn't trust her, in spite of what had happened the previous night. Even though it seemed to confirm what she had told me at our first meeting.

I can play chess, too.

I decided to play along when it came to trust and confidence, play it off the cuff, because if you don't put it down you can't pick it up, and you've got to give a bit to get a bit, preferably a larger bit. Bit is the past tense of the verb to bite, I thought drowsily. So what?

Did Damon and Selin have a snack when they met secretly? I wasn't sure.

Damon was an idealistic kid, and Selin was a Turk, Turks had inherited rigid ideas about women, from way back, when if you fiddled around with a Turkish woman the family got upset, and like as not you'd lose your family jewels, an uncomfortable thought.

Hellena had turned on her side. I glanced again through half-shut eyes at her sun-tanned shoulders and along the line of her figure. She was a fine animal all right. But my last thoughts before I dozed off were of Damon's distraught face when I put the pressure on him, the pain and disappointment and hate, and the sound of his footsteps on the road as he ran after my car in the heat, and weakened in his resolve. I'd won, but I'd held the cards. No satisfaction. It wouldn't have been so bad if he'd been an evil guy. But he wasn't.

We dozed for half an hour, then packed up the picnic things and made our way to the car. We were both silent, satiated with food and wine and sun and each other, but also the matter of Ben Cullon had come between us, though neither of us would have admitted it.

I said I would pick her up the next day but I did not mention a picnic. I suggested we might drive inland, perhaps along the coast in the opposite direction. But if work held me up, she should not wait longer than fifteen minutes, and we would meet the following day. Failing that, I would get in touch by some discreet means. Thus, tacitly, I still seemed to give credence to her story and we parted amicably.

I turned the car round and made towards Rendezvous 3 for my meeting with Damon Nicolaides. I was tired but the drive and fresh air pepped me up.

I knew he would look at me with dark resentful eyes, and I would want to slap him on the shoulder, advise him to tell me to go to hell, admit I'd help him anyway with his American papers, and he ought to realise it. But I knew that he couldn't know it.

He was too young for the poker game. When it came to bluff he didn't stand a chance with me. He was the innocent one.

I wasn't innocent. I was in the mud up to the hocks and

beyond. Ben Cullon was probably playing some devious game. Ahmet the Turk was working for money, and stomach powders, and was involved in VOLKAN. Saleh Karim had his own Middle Eastern machinations. Hellena Christiansen was a question mark shaped like a new animal. Alex Ford hardly counted, a nonentity with a radio transmitter, surfacing occasionally from Hadrian's Wall or the Bignor Roman mosaics.

Damon had been the real idealist, working in AKEL, losing his friends, alienating his family because they thought he had turned Communist. But if he couldn't help himself against me, then I couldn't help him against me.

He was one human unit. With his girl, Selin, it made two units. There were other human units around me, Turkish and Greek, thousands, who would be involved if Demirel were assassinated.

Innocent guys like Nicolaides are defenceless when it comes to a crunch. I knew I had Damon where I wanted him, but my heart was as light as ten pounds of lead, and I was as happy in my work as a vegetarian in a slaughterhouse, yet I had no intention of letting him off the hook.

I had to use him. There was no longer any question of friendship between us. I remembered the hate in his eyes.

I arrived near the rendezvous, four miles outside Kyrenia, fifteen minutes early, and parked the car in a cart-track between an olive grove and some broken thickly-wooded ground, and sat and waited and saw him cycle up and lean his bicycle against a big boulder, and walk towards the car. He was tall and lithe, and was dressed in the narrow dark trousers and coat of a town dweller.

I had liked his friendly open smile when we met before, but as I had expected there was nothing of that today, and when I greeted him he did not reply.

I turned and led the way over stony ground towards a little clearing a few yards square enclosed by tall boulders. It was a hundred yards from the track, according to Frank Baker's map, and on either side, where the ground was less bare, the earth sparkled with yellow fennel and saxifrages and pale pink convolvuluses.

The air was still and warm, and there was no sound except the irregular noise of our shoes on the hard ground and the occasional hum of an insect.

After twenty yards we were out of sight of the track which

in turn had led off a little-used road, ill repaired and pitted with pot-holes.

I suddenly realised that he was very close behind.

So close that once the toe of one of shoes touched the heel of one of mine. I could hear the sound of his breathing and knew that I had been a fool to lead the way, offering him my back.

He was young enough, desperate enough, not to count the consequences of an attack. He was a Levantine who had been betrayed.

I was the betrayer. The one who stood between him and his new life, the enemy, the danger to Romeo and Juliet.

I felt the blood suffusing my face. I was scared and angry. I'd made mistakes in the past, but nothing like this.

I stubbed a foot against a protruding bit of rock-formation, because I wasn't looking where I was going, and swore, trying to think up old routines we'd been taught in the training school:

'AGAINST REAR MANUAL ATTACK. Bend down rapidly, arms between own legs, grasp opponent's leg. Jerk upwards, causing him to fall. Fall on him, winding him.

AGAINST CLOSE REAR REVOLVER THREAT. Swing round, right fore-arm braced, knocking opponent's gun and fore-arm aside. (Time taken for manoeuvre is less than time needed for revolver hammer to be pulled back and released.) If resolutely performed, missile should pass harmlessly by left of body. Do not be shocked by explosion noise. Grapple and incapacitate.'

But what about rear attack with knife? If there was an answer I'd forgotten it.

By the time we were on the threshold of the boulder-screened area where we were to talk, Damon Nicolaides' breathing was heavier. I did not know if this was due to the rising ground or his increasing tension. But it was here, hidden from road or track, that the attack would be made.

I paused and bent forward and slightly to the right, arm outstretched as though to pick a dark blue vetch growing in the grass, and glanced behind me out of the corner of my eye. His hand was moving towards his jacket pocket. Then as he plunged it into the pocket I took a deep breath and attacked him.

It was the usual throw, right thigh behind, and a shove, and he gasped and gave a little cry and went down like a ninepin. You could say with truth it was a proper pushover.

No trouble at all. He lay still.

I pinned his right hand to the ground, sitting astride him, as he looked up at me shocked and bewildered, and felt his jacket pockets. There was no gun or knife in them.

All he had in his right hand pocket was a tatty blue and white packet of his ghastly cheap Greek cigarettes. I got up and helped him to his feet. He still looked dazed, and I'm not surprised.

I dusted him down and apologised.

'I'm nervy these days,' I muttered. 'I'm sorry.'

He spoke for the first time since we had met.

'If I had wished to kill you I would have ridden up to you and shot you as you sat in your car, and then ridden away, sir.'

He was always polite, but I thought that in addition he was suffering too much from shock to be angry.

We entered the little sheltered enclave and sat down. Greek Cypriots are in normal circumstances very friendly people. If you are forthcoming to them they will instantly reciprocate. I did not think Damon Nicolaides would ever be friendly again. I thought it was going to be brutal prodding all the way in future.

I was wrong. Or so it seemed.

He reached out and picked a little wild cyclamen and twiddled it between the thumb and fore-finger of his right hand.

'Did you see Spiros?'

He nodded, and examined the cyclamen closely.

'Did it go well?'

'It could go well. I am to meet him again tonight. The attack on Mr Demirel will be made, not tomorrow, but the day afterwards. Tonight I am to meet him again. He will introduce me to two other comrades of the IN-AKEL group. He will tell us what has been planned, the exact time, the place, and will give us the weapons.'

'What weapons?'

'He will take us to a house, and give us two Sten guns, and show us how to use them. Also a revolver, in case it is needed. Also a map showing certain houses in Nicosia, which will be used for our escape. They were used at the time of the trouble with the British, and I have heard of such houses, sir, they are connected with each other, and there are small rooms under the floor where men can hide and live for days. Some have been kept secret even to this day, even from the police—because in Cyprus, sir, one never knows,' he added, and for the first time a wisp of a smile crossed his serious young face.

I nodded, because it all figured right. I thought once more that very few assassins are fanatics and willing to die themselves. Most demand a sporting chance of escape. I saw him stir and avert his eyes. He said:

'Sir, this is a very dangerous affair.'

I agreed, but there was no percentage in saying so.

'Not if you play it right.'

'I think the meeting with Spiros was observed by others. I think I was followed afterwards. All the evening. Until I went home to bed.'

'Cypriot police in plain clothes?'

He tossed the cyclamen away.

'Not police, you can tell them. In AKEL we always knew. These were Spiros' people, I think. What I do for you is very dangerous, Mr Carter, sir.'

I tried the breezy, hearty line.

'Well, we've got to be careful, kiddo—no walking through Nicosia arm in arm, none of that sort of lark. It won't last long, you know.'

He tore off a couple of fennel leaves and rubbed them between his fingers and sniffed at them, and said lightly as though changing the subject:

'Selin and I will be very short of money at first, when we go to America.'

If there had been any sound on the horizon, which there wasn't, it would have been the distant sound of the old ear-biting machine starting up its engine. I'd heard it many times before.

The disillusionment of yesterday had gone. Philosophically, Damon Nicolaides was going to make the best of the situation.

'How much money would make you less short of money?' I asked in a casual tone.

He tossed the crushed fennel leaves away and shrugged.

'Selin told me the other day we need a few hundred more pounds.'

The ear-biting machine was warming up nicely. I turned my head away and looked at the top of a boulder, because in these matters there is, as usual, a certain delicacy involved.

'How many hundreds?'

'Selin thought five hundred.'

'Two-fifty might make her *less* unhappy?' I suggested seeing that five hundred would have represented two years' work for him at previous rates.

'She would be disappointed with less than four hundred,' Damon Nicolaides said firmly. I didn't comment for some seconds.

'She's a good girl,' I remarked at length. 'I want to see her happy. I won't refuse her three hundred. Half now, half if Demirel leaves Cyprus alive.'

He thought the offer over for about a minute then said:

'Three-fifty, sir, when Demirel leaves alive. Two hundred if he does. None now.'

I agreed to that. I'd have paid twice as much, and more. I'd saved the British taxpayer a hundred or two, and honour was partially satisfied on both sides, which is all you can expect from Middle East haggling.

We parted soon afterwards, and agreed to meet the next day, in the same place.

He had taken off his coat and tie, and was carrying them when he left. I watched him walk down the track in his dark, narrow trousers. His pointed shoes were clean, but dull, in need of a shine.

A little of the anxiety had returned to his face.

I gave him half an hour to get clear of the rendezvous, and lay smoking and listening to the insects and looking at the little rock-plants, and wondering why the inhabitants of this beautiful island couldn't just live in it, and why some seemed hell-bent on inviting a holocaust of destruction and terror.

I would have to send a signal to Ducane to tell him what was in the offing. And another tomorrow giving, I hoped, full details. Some situations you can handle yourself, in the field, if your agent network is big enough and trustworthy enough. Mine was almost non-existent and there was such a stink of treachery around that I didn't trust any of them, except perhaps Damon Nicolaides, and he was working under pressure and for his own purposes.

The Cyprus police would have to be alerted. But not by me, I couldn't do it without blowing my work to them. Ducane would do it, through normal government channels. But not yet, not until the last possible moment.

I did not doubt the integrity of the local police, but Damon was my agent, I was responsible for his safety, and I was highly experienced in agent work. Maybe they were, too, but I wasn't risking it.

And in the end it would be me who would have to winkle him out of the difficulties he had got into on our behalf, and smuggle him out of the island. I did not yet know how, and had given no detailed thought to the problem.

It was just as well.

I drove back and parked the car in front of the hotel entrance in full view of residents and staff, not in the secluded place at the side where it could be tampered with. During the night the porch and hall lights were kept on, and there was what passed for a night porter. He was old and decrepit, but the knowledge that he was about, and the lights, would discourage people from putting a bomb in a car. Wiring it up is not something that can be done in a couple of minutes.

I despised myself for this unreasoning fear of a car bomb. But a colleague had fallen for it. Miraculously, like Hitler, he had escaped with his life. But it had left its mark—on his body, and on my mind.

I strolled round to Alex Ford's place, had a drink with him, and left him to encode my signal to Ducane. He had left the Roman floor-mosaics of Bignor, and was pottering around Cumae, near Naples, where the Sybilline Oracle was prone to consult the Roman Sacred Books. I have been there; a cold, sunken, dungeon-like place only occasionally, dramatically, pierced by thin rays of daylight. She must have had a gay life.

Back at the hotel, I had a wash and was strolling along to the dining-room from the terrace bar, past the front door, when I saw Ben Cullon come in from talking to a hired-car driver.

He paused on the threshold and I saw his hand go out and rest lightly on a little box fixed to the right on the doorjamb. Perhaps rest is too strong a word. He barely touched it as he went past and along the corridor. You could say that he fleetingly caressed it.

One tucks things away in the back of one's mind, small things you notice, and mostly they are lost and gone for ever, for the very good reason that there is no reason why they should be recalled. But now something surged up from the depths of my memory, with a little flurry and a swirl so slight that it hardly rippled the surface, yet leaving behind it two distinct but tiny circles, as a baby trout will do when playing at catching flies.

The first circle concerned something I had heard, somewhere, sometime, in the distant past. It must have interested me, even though mildly, or it would not have been retained in my subconscious. I could not recall what it was, but it seemed to be connected with a door, and I seemed to remember two people, one of them my father, talking and one saying what sounded like 'as you are' and the other replying, 'no, as *you* are'. It was all a long time ago, when I was a kid, and concerned pronunciation.

The second circle concerned a casual remark made by Frank Baker on his way to the airport. He was speaking of Ben Cullon's accident, how it had slightly scarred his face, and left him a little lame, but one didn't notice the lameness much, except when he ran up the hotel steps. Then he might pause at the top to steady himself.

But I had just seen him walk slowly and easily up the steps, and put out his hand not to steady himself, but for some other reason. The lightness with which he had touched the little oblong box glued to the door post was hardly heavier than that bestowed upon a flower by a butterfly before it passes on.

I turned aside and went to the doorway and stood there, as though contemplating some new arrivals who had just driven up.

They passed me and went to the reception desk. I looked at the box. It was very small, perhaps three inches long and one inch wide. It was oblong and painted white like the rest of the door. But the paint seemed whiter than that on the door, as though applied at a later date.

As far as I could see the box served no useful purpose at all.

I examined it more closely and put my hand on it, testing it. It was solidly attached and had no opening, lid, or panel, and there were no obvious wires connecting it to anything. You get microphone minded when you work for Ducane's lot, but unless Cullon wanted to hear the comments of guests ruefully examining their bills as they departed, there didn't seem much point in having a microphone there.

I should have guessed it was the wrong time to show an

interest in the box, should have known that Ben Cullon would probably come popping out to greet some new arrivals. He always did when he could, because he said it made them feel welcome, and a guest who feels welcome starts in a good mood to spend money. He never missed a trick in that way.

'Not planning to steal the lucky scarab, I hope!'

His voice behind me and the hand he laid lightly on my shoulder startled me. I didn't know what the hell he was getting at.

'Scarab, what scarab?'

'Inside the box,' he said, tapping it gently. 'Sammy the Lucky Scarab, Mark 2, said to be an improved model. Guaranteed to be from the tomb of a Pharaoh, like Mark 1. Personally, I think they were both made in Birmingham, but Marion got real upset when Sammy the First was stolen. He is supposed to be a sort of house mascot, which is why a Pharaoh might have one or two stuck in what was going to be his grave, his last home, as it were. To keep him happy you give Sammy a pat now and then. You watch Marion, you'll see her do it now and then, you just watch,' he said, and laughed.

'I wouldn't have thought she was superstitious.'

'I guess most people are superstitious about something. With Marion it's scarabs. It could be worse, I suppose.'

On impulse I decided to challenge him.

'I've seen you do the same as Marion.'

For a moment a thoughtful look came into his eyes, and then it was gone and he was doing the overgrown embarrassed schoolboy act. He shrugged and shuffled.

'Well, you know how it is, it pleases Marion—anything for a quiet life, I guess.'

The act didn't impress me. I thought it was phoney. He turned aside to prop up a sagging geranium in a tub by the door and said:

'You notice things, don't you?'

'I'm paid to. Any idea who stole the first one?'

'Me, Ben Sherlock Holmes Cullon, I narrowed the suspects down to twenty-one,' he said sardonically, 'then the steam kind of petered out. I reckon it was one of a party of British tourists who left the hotel on the morning of April the 25th last year, which was Marion's birthday. It was a good start to the day. Happy birthday, dear Marion, happy birthday to you, and your lucky scarab's been snitched as a start to the morning.

'I reckon somebody came down during the night. We didn't have a night porter in those days. We used to tell people about it. And it wasn't as firmly fixed as now. Anybody could have wrenched it off, whereas now you'd need a pick-axe or a charge of gelignite. There was nothing we could do about it, short of searching everybody's luggage. Sammy was a goner. Marion was certainly pretty upset, I tell you, and I had to rustle around smartly and get another.'

'How the hell do you go about getting a sacred scarab in Cyprus?'

He gave the geranium a final adjustment and swung round. He looked surprised at the question.

'You joking? If you want a pound of hashish, or a couple of camels, or a harem of girls, or a chip off a pyramid, or a sacred scarab, who do you go to? Mr S. Karim, of course, he's the guy for the job.'

Behind us, a tourist woman was querying something. He excused himself and went over to the reception desk. A couple of minutes later he joined me as I moved to the dining-room. They way led past his office and as we were about to pass it, he said, 'Hey, fella, I'll show you something,' and drew me into the little room, and sat down at his desk and opened a drawer.

I watched as he fumbled around and pulled out a pile of snapshots and looked through them. He selected one and tossed it across. It was of himself, taken full face, a good picture, even showing the scar on his face caused by the accident.

'That's me,' he said unnecessarily. 'I printed another one, passport size, and here it is.'

I looked up. He had taken two passports out of his desk drawer. One was Canadian, one British. He shoved the British one across to me.

'That's me again,' he said, grinning broadly. 'A sort of experiment, to see how easy it is to do.'

I turned the pages slowly, passing my finger behind the passport photo, noting that nobody had pricked the paper. He had even filled in the part which asked for identifying marks: *Scar on left of face*. But he hadn't attempted to change the name. The name was still W. A. Anderson.

I looked him in the face and said: 'There was a W. A. Anderson who would have been on Frank's plane if he hadn't cancelled.'

He didn't flicker an eyelid. Maybe he expected the challenge.

'You sure it was *W. A.* Anderson?'

'Dead sure.'

He gave an imitation of whistling to show astonishment, stared at me wide-eyed, and said:

'Well, what do you know! Some guys are born lucky! There's this gink probably cursing himself, postponing the trip because he'd lost his passport, and now is he glad! Boy, is he glad!'

I smiled, and handed the passport back.

'You've made a good job of it. I think passports are a waste of time. How did you get it—from Karim?'

'You name it, Karim's got it. Frank told me about the racket, of course.'

I felt a bit hollow inside. Frank Baker didn't seem to have held much back.

'You can keep it, if you like,' he said. 'Send it to your authorities.'

He held it out to me. I shook my head, saying it would need too much explanation, perhaps cause enquiries and complications. I expected him to put it back in his desk, but he didn't.

'Okay,' he said cheerfully, and ripped it apart and tore up the pages, and threw the lot into his wastepaper basket. 'Now for some dinner. Marion and I have got to go out to some people for coffee later.'

I went to my own table by the window, overlooking the sunset, the rocks, and the sea. To me, Greek and Greek-Cypriot food is uninteresting, apart from the fish and the kebabs, and I had an omelette with a tomato and cucumber salad, and some biscuits and cheese and a glass of beer.

On the face of it, he had disposed of two points, the oblong box and the matter of the passport. I should have been reassured.

I wasn't. I was more uneasy than ever. It was all too slick and facile.

You develop antennae in this work, and it is not possible to describe how they act. One can only say that they waggle around, picking up a faintly false tone here, and a slightly exaggerated gesture there, a lowered glance, or even more suspicious, that frank full gaze which often accompanies a whopping lie.

Thus I was in the same position as Frank Baker before he

died—except that Frank had seemingly come across some fact unknown to me. Had he returned, as he expected, he would doubtless have told me. In his pre-occupation with the safety of Kadem, the Turk, and the haste of his departure, clearly he had decided to postpone telling me what was doubtless a difficult and nebulous story. Cullon must have guessed the position. Perhaps Frank had posted his letter to Hellena in the hotel postbox.

Something had alarmed Cullon enough to let Frank go to his death. If it wasn't something, it was somebody. If it was somebody, it was somebody who was close enough to Frank to report what he was thinking.

For safety he had to assume that Frank had told me of his suspicions. So he had to neutralise the suspicions. Hence this evening's performance.

There was another angle which made me think that beneath his open extrovert manner Ben Cullon might be a remarkably subtle operator. When you find that certain suspicions you had about somebody turn out to be groundless it's natural to feel a bit of a heel. There's a backlash.

You trust them even more.

By the time I'd got to the cheese course I was thinking that if I'd been Ben Cullon, it would have been quite a good idea to get somebody to build up a case against me, so that I could demolish it; so that I could emerge as a much wronged citizen; not wearing a black hat, on the contrary, wearing a hat that was whiter than white.

I'd whistle up some fine animal to do it for me. Who better than a fine animal who had worked well for me in the past, reporting Frank Baker's thoughts and views when Frank visited Athens?

I didn't need to be psychic to pinpoint the animal.

One might think that having seen where Frank Baker's snacks had got him, namely into the Mediterranean sea from a height of about 25,000 feet, I might have been put off my appetite. Far from it.

As I thought of her, over coffee, I began to feel quite peckish again. Poor old besotted Frank had had his snacks with his eyes shut. Mine would be wide open. Maybe she was indeed playing the oldest ploy. Two could play at it.

It's the sort of excuse you make to yourself.

Half an hour later, I sat on the terrace by the front door of the hotel and saw Ben and Marion Cullon drive off in their Fiat. They waved cheerfully. I waved back equally cheerfully. I was glad to see them go. When their car had disappeared I went to the reception desk.

A thin undersized clerk was on duty. He had the inappropriate name of Leonidas. He looked about the last kind of person to defend the Pass of Thermopoli, so he was usually called Leo for short.

I went up to Leo and began a rambling story:

'I want to confirm the address of some people I met at a party a year or so ago, I want to send them a postcard, I believe they stayed here last spring or summer, the name is Mr and Mrs Parker-Mainwaring, pronounced Mannering, but spelt Mainwearing, see? Could you look back in the registration book for me?'

He looked bemused, as I expected, and reluctantly began to drag the heavy registration book over to his side of the desk. I put a hand on it and said: 'Shall I look?'

He thanked me for the offer.

I turned back the pages to April the previous year. There were the usual details of guests, Name, Nationality, Address, Date of Arrival, Date of Departure, Room Number. There were a lot of departures on April 25th, as Cullon had said. All were British except one.

It was the non-British one which interested me. I wouldn't say my heart gave a flutter of excitement or any of that guff, because I'm past that sort of emotion, but I felt pretty keen about the name. It was H. A. RASCHID.

Mr Raschid, whoever he was, gave his home address as something undecipherable, Beirut, and his nationality as Lebanese, which didn't mean he necessarily lived at the address given, or even in Beirut, in fact I thought he probably didn't.

He had arrived on April 23rd and left on April 25th and had occupied the room I was in, which was probably a coincidence. I attached no importance to it at that moment.

I walked out of the hotel and the clean air was welcome after the atmosphere of intrigue which in my mind now surrounded the hotel. I reckoned it was Mr H. A. Raschid who had taken the little oblong box with him, not a British tourist in search of a souvenir.

Again I strolled along to Alex's house. He didn't seem too pleased to see me. He had abandoned Cumae and was now bumbling about among the sulphurous cinders which had buried Pompeii after a Vesuvius eruption. I suppose he thought two signals to London in a matter of hours was a bit much. But I was eager to know if Raschid was known to Ducane.

I sat around until the routine midnight transmission from London came through. I did not tell him of my thoughts about Cullon. He would only look at me in a bemused kind of way, staring at me with faded blue eyes in the pink smooth face, and I would hear his brain going tick-tock, tick-tock, as he tried to understand the implications. I had not even told him about my visitor of the previous night.

His comment in both cases would probably be the same as when I had handed in my first signal about the Spiros IN-AKEL conspiracy. He had looked at it disinterestedly and sighed and said, 'Yes, well, it's all very difficult, isn't it, I'm sure I don't know what one can do about it.'

I tried to discuss a Greek–Turk incident the previous night on the Nicosia–Limassol road, but we never got off the ground, so we said little, awaiting the midnight radio call. When it arrived it was the usual blend of cold practical remarks, with a sarcastic sting in the end. It read:

'Your signal No. 13571 of urgent interest and importance. Await details.

Your signal No. 13572: Congratulations on unearthing name H. A. Raschid, R.I.P. Disappeared night April 25/26 Famagusta–Beirut boat presumed dead, possibly murdered. Raschid was Karim's predecessor. Awaiting further remarkable discoveries—Ducane.'

A scarab, however lucky or sacred, wasn't worth a murder.

Whatever was in the oblong box it wasn't a scarab. Nor was it a microphone. You can buy them two-a-penny these days.

Whatever it had been, it was worth as much as, or more than, the life of H. A. Raschid, either for its intrinsic worth or possibly because it presented a grave threat to Ben Cullon. Threat of what? And if a threat, why was it retained, stuck to a wall? Why didn't Frank Baker know about it, why hadn't Raschid, Karim's predecessor, told Frank about it?

I could guess a likely answer to the last query.

These sleazy bit-piece secret agents like Raschid and Karim have their own side-lines. Maybe they're straight with you and maybe they aren't. Maybe they tell you everything.

Maybe they don't.

I said goodnight to Alex Ford and returned to the hotel. When I arrived I had an unpleasant shock.

Chapter Ten

Ben Cullon was there to greet me. Marion had gone to bed. He said he was sorry to bother me, but he had some people arriving by an early morning coach next day, and could I move my car from the front of the hotel round to the garages at the back. It would make things easier for unloading baggage.

Did I mind? He had left a garage clear for me. No charge, of course.

I thought, yes, and clear for anybody else, and the old bomb fear crept quickly around my heart and into my stomach. I tried to put on an act, but maybe it wasn't convincing enough. He seemed to detect something in my manner, because he asked again, was I sure I didn't mind?

Oh, no, I said, certainly I didn't mind. Not at all.

'Dead easy,' I added, and regretted the word dead as soon as I'd said it.

I drove the car round to the garages at the side of the hotel. One of them had the doors open, with the light switched on inside, sort of welcoming and friendly. It was one of a row of eight. It was also the furthest one from the hotel and the one where anybody entering it would have the least chance of being seen.

What's more, if there were to be a big bang in it, then being the furthest away it would be less likely to damage the hotel windows. I reckoned Ben Cullon would be prudent and economical enough to think of that.

I was glad I was not to be charged for it. I reckoned it would be a big consolation in the next world, or even if I were blinded and scarred. It wouldn't have cost me a cent.

So I drove the car in and locked it, and a fat lot of good that was. Then I tore the spindly end of a flowering shrub off a nearby bush, and stripped it of all its leaves except one, and shortened it, and lightly wedged it under the garage doors. Not so firmly as to call attention to itself if somebody opened the doors in the night, but firmly enough not to be budged by a breeze or a passing cat.

There were always two or three small, thin cats around the back, moving about looking hungry. Hoping to find a loose dustbin lid, I suppose, and get at the remains of the bony red mullet which guests had abandoned in despair. All Mediterranean-type cats are small and thin, and it's not surprising, if they rely on mice and red mullet.

I wanted to go to my room and brood, but Ben Cullon button-holed me for a brandy in his office. He was hanging around waiting for the tourist coach to arrive. I could hardly refuse. We chatted for a while.

He seemed a thoroughly nice guy, apart from possibly being a member of a hostile Intelligence service and a killer.

But he certainly had the old anti-semitic kink, good and proper. You could say he was riddled with the disease. It came out again when I asked him what he thought of Saleh Karim.

'I like him very much,' he replied.

'Why? He's a spiv—useful, I suppose, but a spiv.'

'He's an Arab from the Lebanon, but the main thing is he's an Arab. He's opposed to the Jews, that's good enough for me.'

'Opposed to the *Israelis,*' I said gently.

'Jews,' he said.

His voice had gone all metallic. So had his face. He wasn't relaxed any more. He was sitting upright, alert, armoured for battle.

His mouth was a straight line, lips compressed, even the skin of his face seemed to have tautened. He didn't look handsome. It is strange how hate can take away good looks. But I wasn't going to give him battle, at least not on the lines he anticipated.

You can't convert these guys, you just have to learn to live with them.

When I said nothing, he produced all the old spiel about sinister influences and vice and rackets and all that malarky, ending with the usual generalisation that they are 'everywhere'.

When he stopped I said, 'Well, they're not as everywhere as they used to be everywhere. There's about six million less, give a million take a million. I once forced myself to watch a Jewish family going to the gas chambers.'

That shook him.

'You saw one going to the gas chambers?'

'That's right. A mother and father, a girl, and a kid of about eleven, a boy. And a lot of others, of course, but I was watching this family, they were at the end of the procession, so I could see them better. They were walking in line, hand in hand, all four of them, the parents in the middle, the little boy holding his mother's hand, the girl holding her father's. I saw the father saying something to his wife and smiling, and she nodded and smiled, too. They'd all been told they were going to have their clothes de-loused and fumigated, because naturally the Nazis in charge didn't want to have a lot of panic with people rushing around screaming, they wanted the job made easy. That's understandable, isn't it?'

He was staring at me, face blank and expressionless.

'Go on.'

'Do you want me to?'

'If you want to get it out of your system.'

I took a swig of brandy and smiled in a friendly sort of way, and said:

'It's not in my system, it's in yours. But I guess we're not talking about the same thing. There's not much more to tell. How can there be?'

'Go on.'

'Well, I don't think the father really believed his cheering words to his wife. And I don't think the wife did either, not really. There were an awful lot of guards for a simple, peaceful de-lousing parade, and the building looked unusual. Still, there was always a chance, so she was smiling back at him, to cheer him up in his turn, and anyway they had to put a show on for the kids, whatever they thought in their hearts. Didn't they? I mean, didn't they, Ben?'

He leaned forward to stub out a cigarette and sat back. I said nothing. I wasn't in a hurry. I took another swig of brandy and was glad of it.

'Is that all?'

'More or less. Except that something went wrong somewhere at the head of the procession. I don't know what. Maybe as the first ones were entering the building some guard made a crack, like, "You'll never have no more bugs in your clothes after this!" and looked knowingly at his pals. Witty. Anyway, they had to hustle them in, those first ones. And for a few moments the line slowed down, and I saw a ripple, like a little breeze among corn, as heads turned, and I suppose some words were passed back, and in the middle of the procession some of them started singing, some Jewish religious thing, I suppose, and I think that it was then that the message got through, as it were, and hope died.'

'Any panic?'

He asked the question in the disinterested tone of a police officer enquiring if there had been any trouble among fans queuing to get into a football match.

'Not much. There was this slowing down, and half a dozen made as if to try to break out of the procession, but the others held them back, and the guards had no need to interfere. The singing reached my lot in the end. The father and mother glanced at each other, and faltered a bit, like the rest, then they looked at each other a few seconds, and he put his arm round her waist, and she put her head on his shoulder for an instant, and then they started singing, and the kids joined in, and they shuffled forward.'

'Quite orderly, really?'

'In the circumstances—yes.'

I'm not getting through to him, I thought, not in the slightest, the disease has eaten him up too much. Some leprosy numbs the flesh, this kind numbs the soul. I said:

'At the doors the father took the mother in his arms, and she put her arms round his neck, and he kissed her. Only once, but it was a long kiss. I remember one of the kids said, "Why is Daddy kissing you?"—I think it was the boy—and she said, "Well, because it is my birthday, and he's just remembered, darling." Then her husband said, "Well, I'll just go on and make some preparations," and he touched each child on the cheek, not kissing them, because that wouldn't have been natural and might have scared them, and he walked through the doors ahead of them.'

I stopped and looked at him. He was looking at the floor. But he said, 'Go on,' so I went on.

'The guards gestured to her to follow, so she said, "And as it's my birthday, darlings, I'm going to give you an extra kiss myself," and she picked up each kid in turn and kissed them, and finally said, "And there's some good news for my birthday! Guess what? We're all going to be together again soon, see?" She took each by the hand, and they went through the doors, and the doors closed behind them, like that bit in the Pied Piper of Hamlin, when the Mountainside closes after all the children have entered.'

He looked up at me coldly. Then he made one of the most terrible remarks I think I've ever heard. He said:

'Even rats make kind parents—or so I'm told.'

I looked away, because in that instant his reaction, combined with what Hellena Christiansen had told me, made me decide finally that he was indeed my enemy. But I didn't want him to see it in my eyes.

When I said nothing he asked the question I expected:

'And you, buster? What were you doing when your heart wasn't bleeding? You must have been close to hear that conversation, what were you in the concentration camp? One of the "trusties", one of the prisoners the guards could rely on? What were *you* in the camp, eh?'

I remembered the answer of some gink after the French Revolution, when somebody asked him what he had done during the Revolution. I answered the same way.

'I survived.'

It was a spontaneous, intuitive answer, totally false, utterly different from what I had previously had in mind.

I was going to say that I wasn't there, that I hadn't been captured, which was true; that one night in bed I realised that four brief words, such as 'Six Million Jews Gassed' meant nothing, because you couldn't imagine six million people being gassed. It was just a figure.

So that night I forced myself to watch one family being gassed, and it wasn't true of them all, not by any means, but it was probably true of enough, in its essential details; and then you multiplied it by a million little families, or several hundred thousand families, to be on the safe side; but you got back to the same thing in the end, which was near-insanity.

Counting sheep jumping through a fence, when you're sleepless, is one thing, I was going to say to him, and after a while it is supposed to lead you to slumber; but start imagining a seemingly endless procession of families going to the gas chambers, one member comforting another, and if you persevere long enough you won't be able to sleep because of what you'll call the nightmare horror of it. And then you'll tell yourself that a nightmare is an imaginary thing of the sleeping mind, and this wasn't an imaginary thing.

This was reality, and several hundred thousand horror-realities, repeated one after another in the mind could only lead to madness. But one doesn't wish to invite madness, so one settles for four small words: Six million Jews gassed.

That was what I was going to say but didn't.

He had mentioned me getting it out of my system. I hadn't

got it out of my system. I never will. I wish I had never conjured it up, but it is there for good, ever recurring.

Following my intuition, reversing my plan, elaborating my reply, I looked at him slyly and said:

'I survived—one gets by, one way or another.'

I thought he might have been shocked. But his face was expressionless.

I didn't have to explain what camp I was supposed to have been in, or how I got there, because there was a noise outside, and he turned his head and I saw the coach draw up with the new influx of tourists.

I didn't know whether my intuition had been right or wrong, but at least I hadn't put an end to a short and beautiful friendship. As he got up, I said:

'So you and Saleh Karim, you're on the Arab side?'

He shrugged and made for the door. At the door he said:

'Let's leave it, shall we? But the answer is yes, I am.'

'That puts you on the Russian side, too.'

I thought I saw his eyes flicker slightly, but I may have been wrong.

'Look fella, even the Ruskies can't be wrong *all* along the line, can they? Or can they?'

He gave me one of his broad grins. Full of warmth. Even his eyes smiled. He was a charmer, that boy, except when talking about Jewish people. Maybe he felt that way, or maybe he was just doing a practice run-through of charm, rehearsing the act, before he went out and greeted his new guests.

In bed, I had another of the Walter Mitty sequences. I was back in Ducane's office, telling him I had found the vulture he'd been on about, poor old Frank's vulture. But I knew that if I got down to it there was as yet nothing tangible, nothing I would put on paper in an official report.

You could say I'd caught the Frank Baker disease, when it came to a reluctance to put things on paper.

In bed I lay awake a while, trying to sort things out, and coming to no conclusions. There was a good deal to sort.

I was now convinced that Cullon was not what he seemed, despite the act about the so-called scarab and the passport. The circumstance that Frank's agents had been largely recruited through him pointed to a deliberate attempt to penetrate and control our post in Cyprus. The sole exception seemed to be Damon Nicolaides. But was he? Frank had known his father.

Who had introduced them? I didn't know.

Yet if Cullon were a hostile Intelligence officer set the task of penetrating our Cyprus station, why was Frank not somehow prevented from going on the plane that killed him and Kadem? Cullon was getting all he wanted from Frank. Why kill him?

I thought it possible that Cullon could not stop him without revealing too much of the nature of his own real work. So he let him go. The theory was tenable until I tried to fit in the attack upon myself during the night.

Now I was up against it properly. Spiros Artaxides had seen me arrive. Spiros had watched Frank Baker depart to his death. A man like Spiros had tried to kill me. And a man called Spiros, and resembling him, was involved with IN-AKEL in the assassination plot against Demirel. Spiros was a fairly common name. There might be two involved. And on the other hand there might not.

Cullon could have facilitated the hotel attempt on my life. But it was an odd way to continue the penetration of our Service. I found myself falling back on an earlier theory—that small though it was the order had gone out to liquidate our station. We were in the way, or about to get in the way, of something big.

On balance, it put Hellena Christiansen in the clear.

But nowhere, and by no stretch of the imagination, could I fit in the little oblong box by the door, or the alleged killing of the daring but unfortunate Mr Raschid.

You just don't kill a man because he made off with your scarab, sacred or not, not unless you are a Pharaoh striking from beyond the grave, and that wasn't on, not for my money. So it wasn't a scarab. So what was it?

I put Ben Cullon out of my mind. He was a long-term problem, a strategic problem. Meanwhile, next day, there would be immediate tactical matters to handle.

There was Damon Nicolaides to be seen in the late afternoon. If things were as he said, if his meeting with Spiros had gone as expected, he ought to have the IN-AKEL plans for me, the exact details of the attempt against Demirel, possibly some details of the others involved, and certainly some information about the weapons to be used.

I would have to alert Alex Ford to stand by, and not go out

to a party and just return in time for the midnight radio link-up.

I calculated that allowing for my interview with Nicolaides at five p.m. and getting back to Alex Ford's house, and the time needed to encode the stuff, I would probably be able to get a report off at about seven p.m. The rest was up to Ducane and the Foreign Office and their diplomatic contacts with the Cyprus government and police.

But I would have to house Damon safely till I could get him out of the country. As the newest member of IN-AKEL, he'd come under suspicion when things went wrong. He'd merit words used by magistrates when dealing with young delinquents, he'd be 'in need of care and protection'. A good deal of it, too.

I thought I'd put Cullon out of my mind, but I hadn't. He kept intruding. But it didn't matter. I had time to think. I wouldn't see him again for a while. He always took a day off at the end of the week, Frank had told me so. He and Marion spent it alone.

Sometimes they went for a picnic together. Sometimes they just mooched around the hotel, sitting on their private patio, or maybe he'd spend some time developing and printing his photographs, but anyway they were incommunicado, except in emergencies, and for that I didn't blame him.

Marion was a first-class cook, too. She cooked his meals, and they ate in private, and again I didn't blame him, seeing that it probably saved him the agony of picking his way through the bony framework of red mullet. Mind you, red mullet is a nice fish—what there is of it.

Just before going to sleep, as I imagined, I thought of Hellena Christiansen, and the next day's picnic. I saw no reason to postpone it. It was a pleasant idea to lull one to sleep, thinking of Hellena, or so it seemed. But it wasn't, of course. One thing led to another in my mind, and it didn't induce sleep. It woke me up for a while.

In fact it was back to Ben Cullon in the end and, for some reason, his photographic dark room. In the light of my present opinion of him I had a yen to visit it. Not now, but maybe some other night, when I had nothing much on hand the next day.

Just a quick in-and-out job. A formality, but in this work the more ends you tie up the better. It narrows things down. And it guards your back, so that if anything goes wrong you don't have Ducane looking at you with a mirthless frog-like smile, asking why you didn't do this, that, or the other.

I knew it was locked, because it was situated at the end of the corridor where my bedroom was, and I'd seen Ben walking towards it jingling a bunch of keys. He wouldn't want a guest or chambermaid blundering in while he was developing, and it's no use relying on a notice saying PRIVATE. It won't keep out blundering holiday-makers who've been on the bottle, especially as there was a lavatory next door.

I reckoned he was right to keep it locked.

But I wondered what kind of lock it was, and kept on wondering, so that in the end I put on my dressing-gown and strolled along to have a look, and was glad of the lavatory next door as an excuse if some hotel guest saw me. I had my own bathroom but nobody except the staff knew that.

It seemed to be a simple Yale type lock. A lot of stories get around that it's easy to open these locks—with a piece of mica or something. Well, it's not that easy.

But I went to bed content. I had enough small simple things with me to cope with that lock in less than a couple of minutes if the need arose.

And it did.

I had a bad beginning next day, a shadow of things to come.

I went for a swim before breakfast and that was fine, under the blue sky and sun; and the sea was calm and exhilarating, and there was only one other couple in the water, and they kept their distance, as is proper. Everybody should keep their distance from me before breakfast.

I had a quick rub down, and put on my towelling jacket and lit a pipe and strolled back to the hotel by way of the garages and passed garage No. 8, and saw the doors closed. But the branch with its one leaf was a couple of feet away from where I had wedged it the previous night. The leaf looked sad. Somebody had been into the garage.

It took the gold and the glint off the morning. A day which had dawned with a feeling of zest for the challenges it offered was now suddenly darkened.

So all right, somebody had sneaked in there to see what he could nick from the car; or somebody had gone in early to sweep the place down; or somebody had done something else, or some darned animal had played with the branch and dragged it out from under the garage doors.

But I looked down at the branch with its faded leaf and felt the old sick fear stirring up the stomach nerve-centres. A bomb had sent Frank Baker crashing into the sea. I had seen what a car bomb had done to a brother officer. Somebody had tried to kill me in my hotel bedroom—not with a bomb, but it showed that somebody didn't love me. I thought again: I do not mind the idea of death, but I do not want to be mutilated or blinded.

I was sickened, as so often, by the idea of groping around, first in a world of pain and darkness, and claustrophobic panic; then in a world of no pain, but darkness and the same intermittent panic.

I went indoors and shaved and dressed slowly, trying to concentrate on the coming picnic with Hellena Christiansen, and animal snacks. But she came a poor second.

In the end I did the only possible thing, and went out and stared at the car, and put the key in the door lock and took a deep breath and opened the door. I did cover my eyes with my left fore-arm.

Inside, turning the ignition key to start was always a different matter. If there is a bang in the enclosed interior of a car, then there is a bang, and that's that, and you've had it. Pointless to cover your eyes then. You won't need them any longer.

Nothing happened. I was off beam. But not all that much.

The picnic was a cool, pleasant affair, nothing torrid. Although I no longer regarded her with suspicion, I didn't tell her anything more about anything. It is not in my nature to be gabby, not like poor Frank Baker.

Afterwards, I dropped her off near her hotel in the normal way, but I made no date for the following day. I had an idea I was going to be busy, and anyway patterns of behaviour are to be avoided. In my profession, they can lead to disaster; in private matters of disappointments and heartache.

I had picked her up at noon. By two o'clock I was back at my hotel. It was a quick picnic. She was disappointed. So was I. I could have lazed another hour or two on the sand, in the shadow of the rocks, soaking up the warmth and listening to the whispers of the wavelets. It was one of those idyllic days with a hot sun but enough breeze just to stir the sea at the water's edge.

I could have dozed away that afternoon easily.

The wish was there, the conditions were right, and my rendezvous with Damon Nicolaides was not until five o'clock. But I was uneasy. At heart I knew I shouldn't be there at all, I should have been at my hotel, at my headquarters, easily accessible to anybody who wanted to get in touch with me.

So I was back there in the early afternoon, leaving the car in front of the hotel, walking out of the brilliant sunshine into the sombre coolness of the vestibule, glancing casually at the pigeon-hole above which my room key was hanging, and in which any letters for me would be placed, not expecting to find any, but seeing a folded sheet of paper, a standard form for telephone messages.

It was a casual message, saying that the book I had ordered was ready for collection in Nicosia at my convenience, and meant in fact that Ahmet Aksu wanted to see me, and not at all at my convenience but immediately.

I looked at the big white-faced clock above the reception desk, calculating distance and time and the character of Ahmet.

Allowing for about thirty minutes with Ahmet, I could be in Nicosia and back in time for the meeting with Nicolaides. Assuming the calculations were over-optimistic, as calculations usually are, I might be half an hour or so late for the rendezvous with Nicolaides. That did not matter. An agent will wait three-quarters of an hour for his controller, and vice versa. It is not encouraged, but it is a tacit arrangement. So Nicolaides would wait if necessary. In view of the information he would presumably have with him, he would probably wait longer.

But how seriously should I take Ahmet's message?

There was no doubt about the answer. I had met him only once, but I had judged him to be an easy going, honest Turk, fatalistic, tolerant in most ways, eager for a quiet life, currently interested in three things—survival, money to help in surviving, and stomach powders. Therefore not one to call upon me unnecessarily.

Moreover VOLKAN had its own secret leads into the jungle. What Ahmet had to say might complement Nicolaides' information. So I had no hesitation in gambling on the time element, and went out to the car and took the road out of Kyrenia to Nicosia.

The afternoon United Nations convoy was assembling at the check-point as I went by; outriders, armoured vehicles, buses, to shepherd the Greeks through the Turkish zone to Nicosia.

In Nicosia, Damon Nicolaides would be embarking in the United Nations convoy coming to Kyrenia.

We would certainly pass each other, and I wondered whether he would spot my car and wonder why I was going in the opposite direction to our rendezvous. If he did see me, I assumed he would guess there was a good reason for what I was doing.

As before, I parked near the great mosque that was formerly a cathedral, and Ahmet led me into the room behind the shop and produced coffee, dark and sweet, in tiny cups. He was looking cheerful. It was the first time I had seen him look cheerful.

Once or twice he smiled mysteriously to himself.

I told him I couldn't stay long and he said he wouldn't detain me long. Even when I said I had not had time to get his special stomach powder, he just shrugged as though it was of little account.

He was dressed in the same dark suit I had seen him in before, and his skin was still almost as grey as his eyes but there was an air of self-satisfaction about him. When he had filled the cups he did not sit down but wandered off to the shelves where the guide-books were piled and slowly picked some up and blew some dust off them. It had become a habit.

He was clearly bursting to tell me something and savouring the situation. Finally, he moved to another shelf, and stood there, stocky and square, his back to me. I took a sip of coffee and said nothing. At last he said without turning round:

'Mr Carter, I think your life has been saved and also that of Mr Demirel.'

I put down the coffee cup and stared at his back.

He swung round and looked at me with a triumphant smile on his normally stolid face. Maybe he was thinking that the news justified the money he had been receiving for some time in exchange for very little information. I guessed he might even be about to imply that he had had a hand in the matter of saving my life, so what about a nice dab in the fist? Say, £100? I did him an injustice, but not knowing this, I played it cool.

'Well, that's fine. Who told you?'

'A friend,' he said, and sat down and picked up his coffee cup and took a sip.

He was doing a fan dance, of course, egging me on. I was bored by it, but I dutifully made a grab at the fan.

'What friend?'

'A friend in VOLKAN. He also has a friend.'

'In VOLKAN?' Ahmet nodded.

'In VOLKAN, yes. And he has a friend in AKEL, who has a friend in IN-AKEL.'

I played dumb bunnies, looked at him blankly, said: 'IN-AKEL?'

'Last time I told you of a new little group—it is called IN-AKEL.'

'It is?'

'That is its name. This person in AKEL tells things to the friend of my friend in VOLKAN. Thus one learns of things.'

'For VOLKAN money?'

He shrugged, said evasively:

'Yes and no.'

I wasn't letting him off the hook. I wanted to know, because information given for money, cash down, can be different from information given out of friendship. The truth content can vary by about 100 per cent.

'Either it was for money or it was not,' I said bleakly.

He looked at me pityingly.

'Mr Carter, I see you don't know the Eastern Mediterranean—things aren't always done for money alone, no indeed, the wise man will take money for today and bank friendship for tomorrow. Today the Greek Cypriots are in power, but with Turkey only forty miles away, who knows about tomorrow? Turkish friends could help. These thoughts can occur, even to a Communist Greek Cypriot in AKEL, if he is prudent, for nobody can say what the future holds.'

I wasn't impressed. I thought it more likely that some Turk in VOLKAN had got some dirt on a high-up AKEL Communist who knew about IN-AKEL, and was twisting his tail till he squeaked. But I wasn't going to get any further with Ahmet about the source.

I nodded and waited, and he put his hands on his knees and looked at me and said earnestly:

'Allah is merciful, Mr Carter.'

I looked at him in surprise. I didn't want to deny the truth of his words, it was just that I had read such words in books, heard them on the screen, but never expected to hear them in real life. I nodded.

'The hand of Allah, the Almighty, the all merciful, can be

observed in the saving of your life, Mr Carter.'

'Then praise indeed be to Allah,' I murmured. 'What's happened?'

'Last night a man was killed who would have killed *you.*'

For a few seconds I said nothing, visualising what I remembered of Spiros Artaxides, whom I had seen at the airport. What exact part he had played in the blowing up of Frank Baker's air-liner I did not know, but intuition told me that Spiros Artaxides, who had almost certainly helped to kill Frank Baker, had probably tried to kill me, and apparently had intended to try again, was better dead.

Too late to help Frank, soon enough to help me.

'Was he of medium height, thick-set build, aged about forty, with a gold ring on the third finger of his right hand? What was his name?'

'I do not know. It will be in the paper tomorrow. VOLKAN had been watching him for some time, Mr Carter. Last night they saw him leave a meeting with other men. He was carrying a case which could have held a musical instrument, a——'

He paused to imitate a man playing a clarinet.

'A clarinet case?'

'That is right, a clarinet case, but later they knew that it did not have a clarinet in it. It had a Sten gun, Mr Carter. They followed him in a car to some big building. He was on foot. You will understand that it is not easy to follow in a car a man who is walking, that you will know. You must stop from time to time, and this he may notice. They think that he did see them, for he looked round now and then, and walked faster.'

That figured. Spiros Artaxides was too cunning an animal not to know when he was being followed in a car. And at night, too, with the sidelights on.

'Why use a car?' I asked irritably. Professional mistakes annoy me. But then these people were comparative amateurs.

'They wished to invite him into the car, to talk to him,' Ahmet said. He smiled briefly.

I remember thinking that I would have liked to have been present when VOLKAN talked with Artaxides. I would have put a few questions myself.

'But there were still too many people in the street to invite him into the car, which was a pity. Therefore the car stopped and two men from the car followed him on foot, one behind the other, with some distance between, and the car followed the last man, and so he did not now know he was being followed. So they followed him to this building and saw him go in, and a light go on in a room on the ground floor, where he lived alone. So they drove up to the door, and decided to go in and invite him to go outside and into the car for this talk.'

It was about now that my intuition began to feel less cocky. I had been aware while Ahmet Aksu rambled on that something was odd somewhere, but because I was listening I did not have a proper chance to think the query through. Now, as he paused, I knew what it was.

If the meeting covered by VOLKAN was one at which Spiros Artaxides gave his final instructions and armed Damon Nicolaides and the other two, then it was strange that Artaxides should have been carrying a Sten gun home himself, *unless somebody had chickened out at the last moment.*

On paper, it was three to one against Nicolaides dropping out because he wanted my money, among other things. That was what I told myself. But I didn't believe myself. I reckoned that the odds were three to one *on* that Damon Nicolaides had thought better of it. The kid had never had a hard core in him. Tough, in some ways, but not iron hard.

Disappointment has a bitter taste, and the greater the affair the deeper the flavour. Ahmet Aksu was rambling on, savouring the story; but I was mentally composing the signal I would have to send Ducane. And I was deeply shocked. He would be expecting details of plans and personalities involved in the plot. Now he'd get nothing, except news that the agent had funked it at the last moment.

I knew I'd get the blame. It would be implied in the politest way that I should have stuck closer to Nicolaides, almost taken him to the meeting with Spiros at the gun point. Ducane, he'd try to defend me, he'd been in the field, he knew what was practicable and what was not, but it's what they'd think higher up, sitting in their office chairs, that depressed me. I heard Ahmet say:

'So they went into his room, though they had to wait for a few minutes until some people talking on the landing above had stopped talking and shut their doors. Then they went in suddenly, one of them with a gun with a silencer.

'He had unpacked the Sten gun, but not loaded it, though this they did not know. It was unlucky for him they did not know this, and unlucky for the VOLKAN men, I think, because in the end they could not talk to him. Also unlucky that when they opened the door without warning, he was holding the Sten pointing at the door, perhaps by accident. So the VOLKAN man with the gun shot him with two bullets, and he died in some seconds, this IN-AKEL plotter. Does one blame the man who shot him? Or does one *not* blame the man who shot him?'

Ahmet looked at me questioningly. He seemed genuinely interested. Me, I didn't give a damn, and shrugged my shoulders, being preoccupied with other thoughts, such as whether Spiro's successor would do a last minute recruitment to make up for the defection of Damon Nicolaides, and whether the plan would go ahead. If it did, I would know nothing of it now. I thought it would. Too much had been laid on, too many plans made, to call it off.

'This I tell you, Mr Carter, to show you that the information I gave you at our last meeting about this little group is true, and also that you are in danger from them, because before he died this IN-AKEL man cried out in Greek which the Turkish VOLKAN men do not understand. But they heard the name Demirel, and also there was something about "Mr Carter", so I think that our Mr Demirel and also you were to be killed by him and may still be by others. I think VOLKAN did well.'

I didn't think so. I was listening to the street noises outside, to a woman talking in a loud voice to Ahmet's assistant in the shop, to some children playing somewhere, the rumble of wheels on the pot-holed street, all the mingled distant noises of Nicosia, and also to the sound of my heart echoing in my head, like slow drum beats thudding out the Christian name of Nicolaides, DA-MON DA-MON DA-MON.

I tried to escape from reality, to give myself time to recover, insisting to myself that the VOLKAN shooting was understandable, recalling a line in one of the Kai Lung books which says approximately, 'When menaced by an approaching tiger, mere flowers of speech are as noisesome bindweed,' and the VOLKAN people felt themselves menaced by an IN-AKEL assassin with a Sten gun.

Thus the brain shied away from what seemed the awful fact, but the heart thuds still sounded in the background, and I felt a flush spreading over my face, and noted Ahmet Aksu looking at me in surprise, and guessed he thought that my emotion was caused by the linking of my name with Hasan Demirel's as a target for assassination.

I banged down the coffee cup noisily, and got to my feet and began to walk about the room, and said angrily:

'I don't think VOLKAN did well, I don't think they did well at all. They should have taken a risk, they should have jumped aside—and then *at* him—there were three of them, and he was only one. He couldn't have killed them all, and now we know he couldn't have killed any.'

He looked at me sardonically, still interpreting my emotion as fear for my own skin.

'I'm not worried about myself, I'm worried about your Hasan Demirel, and this lost chance to grill this—this man that's what annoys me.'

'Naturally,' he said gently. 'More coffee?'

I shook my head, not even saying thank you, and again pressed for a name or description.

'This man they shot—describe him. Was he young, old, middle-aged, tall, thin, fat, and what was his name, any idea of his name? They must have searched his room, they must have known whom they shot.'

Ahmet spread his hands and said:

'Mr Carter, Mr Carter! You do not understand, I have the news from a friend who has a friend—how can I know the small details, they will certainly be in the newspapers tomorrow. Meanwhile I thought that since your own name was mentioned by this IN-AKEL assassin——' He stopped, looking crestfallen.

I looked at his serious, dull face, and felt remorse. He'd expected a pat on the back, and all he'd got was bad temper. I also looked at my watch. I would have to leave if I were to keep the planned rendezvous with Damon Nicolaides. And I would have to keep it.

If he arrived, I knew I would wish to embrace him, place my arms round his shoulders affectionately, overwhelm him with some expression of my joy, which to him would be inexplicable.

He wouldn't know it was caused by relief to the conscience, because a young Greek man, with his life before him, who had tried to break away to marry his Turkish sweetheart, and had been bulldozed back into the battle, had not been wiped out after all.

You don't think these thoughts logically, consecutively,

clearly, it's only in retrospect that you know that such was the sum total of your feelings, in the round, at a certain moment.

I said goodbye to Ahmet, and promised to keep in touch one way or another, and thanked him for his promptitude in the matter, and went out of the dim, cool shop into the warm afternoon sunshine and the dust and noise of the city, and picked my way along the shabby streets of the Turkish quarter to where my car was parked, and climbed in with never a thought of a bomb inside it.

Outside Nicosia, the United Nations convoy, headed by its Finnish outriders looking like begoggled frogmen, was approaching the end of the Kyrenia–Nicosia duty run, headlights blazing, brilliant even in the sunshine, the outriders' arms waving imperiously at oncoming traffic to make way, and make way fast, and get to hell out of it.

I didn't take any notice.

Normally, I would have obediently drawn into the side of the road till the Fast Package and then the lumbering buses and vans of the Slow Package had passed me. But I gauged that Frank Baker's Rover had room, and we passed each other at speed, with disapproving glances from the outriders and defiant ones from me.

I didn't care, because I was feeling better, still uneasy, but seeing the matter in greater perspective. A dying Spiros Artaxides had good cause to link my name with Demirel. Even thugs have a tendency to clear the upper decks of their conscience.

Damon Nicolaides would have thought of Selin, his sweetheart, called out her name, not mine, not Hasan Demirel's.

Thus the cooling late afternoon air, the control of a fast car, the mountains of the Kyrenia pass, and the distant view on the left of Fort St Hilarion calmed me down, till by the time I had slowed to pass through Kyrenia and turned right along the coast to Rendezvous 3 another obvious theory sprang to mind.

IN-AKEL existed, and VOLKAN had covered a meeting of one of its cells. But which one? There was nothing to indicate that Damon belonged to this particular cell. It showed how one could jump to wrong conclusions.

I was greatly relieved now. But it had been a bad period while it lasted.

I wondered whether I ought to tell Nicolaides about it, about

VOLKAN's involvement, and decided that I certainly should. It was essential that he should be on his guard. The last thing I wanted was to have him beaten up by Turkish terrorists. The hold I had on him was tenuous enough already.

A beating up, a stiff interrogation, a threat to his life, might tip him over backwards again, apart from what he might reveal about his link with me. As I turned right along the cart-track that lead to the Rendezvous I thought, as I'd thought before, that there was no hard iron core to the lad.

I had got over my sloppy qualms of conscience, and once more was tough and objective, and this mental state continued even when I saw that his bicycle was not leaning against the tree in the lane where he had parked it last time. I was only five minutes late, and though I would have liked to see it I reflected that either of us could be up to three-quarters of an hour late.

I waited in the car for ten minutes. Then the fear began to creep back. I knew it had never been properly killed, had been just dormant, ready to stir and creep forth when the time was ripe.

Forlorn optimistic possibilities began to creep forth along with the fear, attempting to push it back with their tiny, hopeless strength. The healthiest was that he had had a puncture, had hitch-hiked a lift in a car—had arrived long before me, and gone ahead to the enclave surrounded by rocks where last we had talked.

That one was a really good starter, and I locked the car and took to the rough, stony path, and passed on the way to the enclave the spot where I had swung round on him in suspicious apprehension, and flung him to the ground.

I remembered the puzzled and reproachful look on his face, and would have given a good deal to see it again, indeed any sort of look, because he wasn't waiting for me among the boulders, and fear was back in full strength.

I sat on the rock where I had sat before, and beside me, where he himself had sat, where our feet had trampled the grass and flowers, the vegetation was still bruised, and among it was a blue wild cyclamen which he had picked and now lay faded and shrivelled.

I waited over an hour, thinking of the three meetings I had had with him. Only one had been happy and carefree, the first, illumined by his joy and excitement at the prospect of meeting

Selin. The second had been dreadful, naked blackmail, and I recalled the sound of his footsteps on the hot road as he ran after my car to announce his bitter surrender. And the third had been marred with initial suspicion, violence, and haggling.

I began some bargaining with the Almighty about what I would and would not do for Damon Nicolaides and his girl Selin, whom I had never seen, if only Damon had not been killed. A few moments later I heard a sound and at once I was glad I had signed nothing on the dotted line with the Almighty.

At first, so great was the relief, that I could not believe that there were footsteps on the path, the sound of a stone being dislodged, the crack of a snapping twig. When there was no doubt, I rose to meet Damon Nicolaides, but old habits die hard, and before I walked round the giant boulder which shielded the path I slipped my hand into my pocket and released the safety catch on the Walther automatic, though I need not have bothered.

It is rarely necessary to shoot goats.

The two goats paused and looked at me with pale yellow, slanted eyes, and then turned indifferently aside and wandered off.

I did not sit down again. The light was less brilliant, the day reluctantly fading, and I knew now that Selin, the Turkish Juliet, was widowed before she was ever married to Damon, her Greek Romeo, and I was glad I need not face her. Saleh Karim could break the news.

I went back to Alex Ford's place to send off my signal to Ducane. On the way, I passed Hellena Christiansen's hotel, and wanted to seek her out, relax in her warm personality, and unburden on her some of the guilt I felt.

Useless to tell oneself one did what seemed right at the time, in the light of the circumstances, choosing the lesser of two evils. Useless to hear somebody else say it. I drove past.

The signal to Decane was brief enough: *Agent Apollo killed. No further information.*

It wouldn't take long to decipher, anyway.

Chapter Eleven

Alex Ford shrugged as he took the message for transmission, looked at me with his faded blue eyes, and said, 'Oh, dear—was he important?'

'Not very—not in the long term. But he had a certain value at the moment.'

He shrugged again, and said, 'Bad luck,' and asked no further questions. He just wasn't interested. In a way he was paid not to be interested. Occasionally, no doubt, he surfaced from the mists of the past and the dust of Roman antiquities, but not often enough to be interested in the death of Damon Nicolaides. He was a cog, knew it, and had no ambitions above safe cogdom.

I drove back towards the Thessides hotel, but stopped a couple of hundred yards short of it, under some carob trees. The hotel was brightly lit and some sort of radio music was blaring out of one of the open downstairs windows. I wanted a drink badly, but felt a disinclination to re-enter the world of normality. Cheerful people would depress me further.

The noise of the bar would prevent me thinking, but I wanted to do some thinking, to shake off at least some of the guilt. I had never felt more lonely, and thought again of Hellena Christiansen. I would even have settled for a sight of Ducane's sardonic, frog-like smile. But I had to think things through. The threat to Demirel remained. The job was still on hand.

But now I had no tools for the job.

I sat in the car with the windows open to the warm night. Other cars came and went. There was the usual Saturday-night special entertainment at the hotel. Ben Cullon drove off in his white Fiat, in the direction of Kyrenia, and for some seconds I thought nothing of it. But something was going tick-tock in my mind. I couldn't identify the cause, not until his tail lights had disappeared.

Then I remembered Frank Baker's words. 'He has one day off a week, just mooches about, sits on the patio, or something, never goes out, never meets anybody unless it's an emergency.'

I started the engine and drove to the hotel and put the car in the garage, voluntarily this time. I had an idea that I didn't want Cullon to know I had returned. It was just a passing thought.

I went on foot to Kyrenia, ten minutes walk away, and the water-front cafés, passing the building which was a club for the Canadian unit of the United Nations force. Music was blaring inside, and some of the boys were sitting outside, and some I could see sitting around the bar within. All looking cheerful, raucous, and fit. I envied them.

His car was parked outside a large café halfway towards the old castle which dominated the harbour. It was one of several. He wasn't seated at one of the tables outside, so must have gone inside, out of sight, despite the warmth. I did likewise, in a smaller nearby café.

I didn't know what I expected, or why I was there, and ordered a large gin and tonic. They brought it with the usual dish of nuts and I sat for half an hour, and was halfway through a second gin when I saw his Fiat pass slowly by.

He was alone.

I didn't know whom he'd met or why, and it seemed I could have saved my time. But when I had nearly finished the remains of the gin a short stock figure strolled along the pavement, head bent, staring at the ground, apparently in deep thought.

I didn't know if it was the man who had attacked me in my bedroom. But I did know it was Spiros Artaxides whom I'd seen at the airport when Frank Baker left. There was no mistaking that squat hood, and as he passed the lighted café he lifted a hand to scratch a cheek, and I caught the glint of the light on a gold-coloured ring.

I paid and left.

There was no proof that Artaxides and Cullon had met in the dark corner of a café. There was no proof that they hadn't. But Cullon had broken the pattern of a day when he remained rigidly incommunicado—except in an emergency. What was the urgency? I walked back to the hotel, conscious of a complete information black-out, disquieted and as depressed as before.

I went to the bar and had another couple of slugs of liquor, changing over to whisky this time, because I wanted to, and the idea that mixing gin and whisky makes you more sloshed is a lot of hooey. Spirits are spirits, whether made from grain, potatoes, juniper, or any other form of vegetation. Alcohol is alcohol is alcohol.

Dinner was a leisurely farce, toying with mediocre food, leaving most of it, wishing the small, skinny cats luck unless it was wolfed by the waiters before it got to the cats. The white wine seemed to me warm, overpriced, too sweet, and generally filthy, the coffee tepid, and the service slow and grudging. You could say I didn't enjoy the meal.

After this Belshazzar of a feast I sat in one of the lounges brooding about what to do next and finding no real answer. All that could be done was to cross the t's and dot the i's on what I had sent Ducane already. I had hoped to send so much, the place, method, and timing of the assassination attempt. In the event I had left him out on a limb.

Then I began to pull myself together, to assess what scraps of information I had. I could point to a reasonable theory on timing, and add the name of Spiros Artaxides as a citizen to be watched. Not that he would be likely to be directly involved himself. Doubtless he had killed, tried to kill, and some time would kill again, but I had the feeling he wasn't going to fire the shots on this actual job.

As to the timing, I based my estimate on three points. First, the killers had been armed the previous evening. Second, INAKEL would know that the longer they were hanging around with armaments, the greater the risk of some kind of slip-up. And Demirel was not staying long. Third, they would nevertheless be given time, even a minimum of time, to acquaint themselves with plans and maps, not only for the coup but for subsequent escape. A brief period in which to wander around streets and buildings.

That period of grace could be today, and maybe today alone. Therefore I figured that the attempt might well be tomorrow. I began to jot down the signal to Ducane, cutting out unnecessary words, paring it down to the bone. The signal ended formally: *No restrictions on action.* An officer in the field can restrict action to protect the safety of his agent or himself. It was no longer necessary.

The agent was dead. Admittedly I was alive, but that didn't matter. Good local agents are difficult to replace, people from head office are not. Ducane would look at the words and smile, knowing that it would look good on the file. Good and formal. Punctilious. From the point of view of my future career I was playing from weakness now. Scraping the bottom of the barrel.

Call it what you like. And these small things count.

I strolled out into the warm, scented night air, and along the road to Alex Ford's house. I knew the road well by now—which gardens held lilies, which shrubs, which gave out perfume, and which didn't.

There was no moon, but the stars were bright enough to lighten the darkness, and, because it was so, I thought that although I was surrounded by darkness the darkness was visible. And the words themselves conjured up for a passing moment the interior of a Masonic Lodge, the Master in his chair on a dais, the Wardens in their allotted places, the Brother outside, ferociously armed to prevent outsiders breaking in during a ceremony. As if anybody would want to.

The signal, or the main outlines of it, lay snugly in my breast pocket, I was in no great hurry, guessing that Ducane would already have come to the same conclusions as myself. He was no slouch. But it showed willing.

So I strolled along through the darkness visible, thinking of masonic ceremonies and pleasant dinners devoid of red mullet, and the long schism between the Continental Grand Orient Lodge, with its reputation for atheism and political intrigue, and the British and other Lodges, purely charitable, religious, and social.

Darkness visible ended as I turned in at Alex's gate, and heard it squeak shut behind me, and saw the lights glowing cosily behind the drawn curtains, because he always drew the curtains in an attempt to keep moths out. He hated moths.

I couldn't help pausing and looking at the scene, once again envying him his peaceful life, his gentle absorbing interest in ruins, and, come to that, his regular little salary from us in exchange for a couple of short stand-by periods each day.

I wouldn't have minded ending my working days in that way, I thought, but I never would. That was certain. I remembered the officer in the film about the bridge over the River Kwai, leaning over it, talking to his Japanese captor about his own military career, saying sometimes he just wondered whether it had all been worthwhile, and the Japanese officer looking at him in amazement. Ducane would look at me in the same way, if I ever said such a thing. But I sometimes thought it, though not often, and I thought it now, because in effect I had killed Damon Nicolaides, an innocent who only wanted to escape. The feeling would pass, of course.

It had almost passed as I rang the bell. The radio was on. I guessed, rightly, that he couldn't hear the bell, and made my way round to the back of the house, to the garden door, and so to the living-room, knocking at the door and calling out his name. He couldn't hear that, either, being asleep.

He was sitting in an easy chair with his back to me, an open map of the North African littoral, with its Roman ruins, spread out on his knees, a travel brochure by his side. He was wearing one of the silk scarves he put on in the evening as part of 'changing for dinner'. I thought it was nice to fall asleep, indulged in your hobby, after a nice dinner, and walked round to tap him gently on the knee, because it's bad to wake people suddenly, and he certainly was asleep, as I said, so deeply asleep he wouldn't be needing the travel brochure, either now or ever.

At first I thought it was a heart attack and wrenched the scarf loose, but then I saw the thin broken line round his neck, such as a running wire noose would make and knew what had happened. Like me, somebody had come in through the back garden door.

There are these carotid arteries which supply blood to the brain, and two or three seconds pressure on them and there's a loss of consciousness. The rest is a matter of time, and not much time, either. They tell you about it at training school.

It's quite painless, they say. I wouldn't know.

I didn't loosen the wire, because there was not a vestige of life in him, and several unmistakable signs of death. I was glad the curtains were drawn, because I wasn't going to get involved if I could help it. The radio was quieter now. An English B.B.C. voice, somewhere, was mumbling on about irrigation in Lower Egypt or something. I sat down on a hard chair for a couple of minutes to recover from the shock, and then pulled myself together and got up before some sort of reaction set in.

On a conservative estimate it would take fifteen minutes to encode my signal to Ducane, and send it on the priority wave, and I quickly made my way to the safe and the closet under the stairs, where Alex kept the transmitter and code books. I had the spare key and the combination lock sequence, but I didn't need them.

The place was empty, and I might have expected it.

Back in the living-room, I wrapped my right hand in a

handkerchief to obviate finger prints, and pulled open the drawers of the writing desk and tipped the contents on to the floor. Then I began to go through the bungalow, to do the same to any chests of drawers I came across.

A police officer once told me that police, alerted by a neighbour, often failed to search a house properly for a criminal who was possibly still hiding there, having been surprised upon the premises. There was not much to search in the bungalow. A bedroom, a bathroom, the kitchen and larder, but I wasn't happy.

The bedroom door was closed. I kicked it open, and stood quickly aside and put a hand round to switch the light on. The room seemed empty.

But the door of a built-in wardrobe on the far side was slightly ajar.

The hair on the back of my neck tingled as I approached it. It, too, was empty. So was the bathroom. I put the Walther automatic back in my pocket.

In the end it looked reasonably like a normal burglary, and I left, the lights still on, the radio still playing, and Alex Ford still, in general, suitably dressed for dinner.

Outside, reaction really set in.

I leaned against the wall to recover. I wasn't actually sick. But I felt pretty weak at the knees, and stared out into the darkness visible, at the stars and the blue-black sky and the outline of the trees and shrubs.

I was wondering if Cullon had received the news of Nicolaides' death some hours *later* than I had; if Ahmet therefore had finally, unwittingly. without much effort, justified his salary by reporting to me so promptly—and I wondered if Cullon had tried to stop me sending the news of Damon's death, or any other news, reckoning that London would take no action pending another report from me, which wouldn't come, which couldn't come, since Alex was a goner, and his transmitter, too.

So London would wait, so no action would be taken, so the coup would go forward.

I remember I clenched my fists, not against some physical threat but against the onslaught of contradictions on the mind, trying to grope a way through yet another one: if Ben Cullon had arranged the killing of Damon Nicolaides, he wouldn't have needed this hasty last-minute operation, this meeting on the harbour front on his day off work.

So it was unexpected, a genuine VOLKAN job, and the killing of Alex Ford was an urgent last minute off-the-cuff operation, a hasty re-adjustment of a careful plan.

Frank Baker's vulture, if Cullon was the vulture, had been caught on the hop. No contradiction there. Vultures did hop towards their meat. They didn't walk like starlings, but hopped, heavily, towards a carcase.

I'm no vulture, at least not much of one, and I didn't hop heavily back towards my hotel. But I walked heavily towards it.

At a cross-roads a hundred yards from the building there was a lighted telephone kiosk. I paused by it, tempted to ring Hellena, but decided against it, because it was pointless, a self-indulgence, surrendering to a desire to off-load some of my guilt by talking to her.

I trusted her now, I was not surprised that Frank Baker had confided in her, and I didn't think he'd died because he had done so. But I didn't want to burden her with my secrets or my worries. She didn't deserve the burden and had said she didn't like secrets.

Fifty yards from the hotel I stopped to light a cigarette, because I smoke everything, pipe tobacco, cigarettes, cigars, bits of old carpet, anything, and I know I shouldn't, that it's madness, but I do. As I fumbled for my lighter I saw Saleh Karim's car draw up in front of the hotel, and his pear-shaped figure struggle out of the driving seat and waddle towards the hotel entrance.

You can't rightly call a stout man like Karim a shadow, but I thought of him as such. I had only been on the island a few days, and they were all still shadows to me. I didn't know them in depth, because Frank had died too soon.

Karim was a shifty passport-smuggling shadow, willing to turn his hand to anything. Ahmet Aksu was a dour, phlegmatic Turkish shadow, with stomach pains and a shop containing dusty books and tourist guides.

Selin was only a shadowy name.

Damon Nicolaides was no shadow, he was a guilt-laden burden on me, but I didn't really know him, and Alex Ford was as much a nonentity dead as he had been alive.

I couldn't fit Spiros Artaxides into things, but I thought I knew my vulture and to some extent what was in his mind.

Frank Baker had gone. Alex Ford had gone, Nicolaides had gone. I myself was now cut off from radio communication with Ducane. We were getting thin on the ground. And the ground was isolated.

As I watched Saleh Karim waddle into the hotel, thinking that this day there was certainly a gathering of the clan, I knew, or thought I knew, who was the biggest shadow.

It was Hasan Demirel. First, it had been Mahmoud Kadem, now it was Demirel. Each was as shadowy as the other, but each was an emissary of peace, a living symbol of better things, distracting our attention, so that slowly we were being picked off, so that in the end Ducane's station in Cyprus would fold up.

I saw the hotel swing-doors close behind Saleh Karim, and speculated again about why Saleh, a prosperous trader, should have been willing to work for Frank Baker, even to the extent of driving on errands for him, transporting Nicolaides' girl Selin during her short, sad courtship.

I was in no doubt that he was engaged in some double agentry, playing both ends against the middle, and that was dicey around these parts. But now I wondered why he had been summoned by Ben Cullon. Given the time and circumstances I felt sure he had, in fact, been summoned, and wasn't just popping in for a chat.

I didn't rate him a good insurance risk.

That would leave Ahmet Aksu, deeply ensconced in the Nicosia Turkish sector, not easy to get at. It also left me.

I could be replaced in a few hours, maybe by some keen rosy-cheeked young chap eager to win his spurs. But it takes a long time to build up an agent network. The more I thought of the past set-up the more amazed I felt. Directly or indirectly, Frank had made most of his contacts through Ben Cullon. He thought he was discreetly controlling Cullon. It was the other way round. I began to wonder whether even Alex Ford was all he seemed, since he'd been suggested by Cullon.

Now, for some reason, Cullon seemed to have had orders to clean up the network. Finally. Leaving no records and nobody to squeak. Alex's transmissions could have been monitored, even if he were in the clear. Cullon might well guess that Frank's suspicions and mine were nowhere at present on paper.

Frank was dead. Mine were in my head.

A little gusty breeze ruffled the leaves of the trees, and there was a cool edge to it, at least for me, because I was thinking of the note Hellena had sent to my hotel when she first made contact. I could visualise the sentences in her bold but feminine handwriting. The note had exuded a pathetic, amateurish attempt to get in touch with me discreetly, even secretly. If Ben Cullon had read it, and I had to assume he had, he might have done some deep thinking about Hellena Christiansen.

I had been so preoccupied with Nicolaides and the others that I had forgotten about it. Cullon wouldn't have done. I now believed that beneath that boyish gaiety was a cool retentive brain capable of anything from murder to overcharging for orange juice. You could say I didn't like the guy any more.

I walked quickly back to the telephone kiosk and rang Hellena, and asked her to meet me on the beach, among the rocks, where we had first met, in about thirty minutes time. She sounded pleasantly surprised, poor girl, and agreed readily enough.

I called at the hotel, picked up a hundred pounds from the money Frank had left me, and arrived among the trees above the meeting-place, looking down at the group of rocks among which we had sat.

From here I could see the steps from the hotel which she would use, and also the surrounding beach, and the rocks among which she would pick her way. I couldn't see all round the boulders, of course, and there were a good many deep shadows, because now there was a three-quarter moon, but it would be insane for anybody to try anything during that short walk, at such short notice. Or would it?

I suppose I was getting neurotic about the whole situation. I'd never lost an agent before Nicolaides, or colleagues at such short intervals as Frank Baker and Alex Ford, and I didn't want to lose anybody else. So I over-reacted, sitting there with the Walther automatic, knowing I couldn't hit people at that distance, because automatics have only short-range accuracy, but I could distract their attention.

I saw her come down the steps, and from the shape of her dress it seemed to be the same yellow one she had been wearing when we first met. She picked her way along the beach and sat down on the boulder where we had sat before, looking around, expecting to see me, perhaps surprised I wasn't there, perhaps uneasy.

I clambered down to the beach, and called her name when I was a little way off, so as not to alarm her, and then approached and sat down beside her on the ledge.

I didn't kiss her, or even put my arm round her. It wasn't a time for animal snacks. But I put a hand over hers, and spoke earnestly and at some length, telling her everything, concealing neither facts nor theories, cutting out wisecracks, cynicisms, empty bravado, and even mentioning my earlier doubts about her. She released her hand and said:

'It's a dismal picture. Why are you telling me now, here, so suddenly?'

This was the point of no return, so I looked her in the face and came out with the truth:

'Because I want you to check out of the hotel tomorrow. In the morning. Early. And leave Cyprus.'

She looked startled and dismayed.

'Go back to Athens?'

'Not Athens—London. Get in touch with Ducane. Tell him all I've told you, what Frank told you, what you think, I want him to know. Don't you see,' I went on urgently, 'don't you see there's nothing on paper yet, no report at all, and I have no radio communications now. At first there were only suspicions in Frank's mind and yours—and then in mine. Now there's only you and me. There's another reason, too. I'd be happier, personally, if you were safely away from this place, where there's so much hate.'

I took a deep breath and added:

'We agreed we wouldn't fall in love and all that malarky. And I'm not. But I'm getting a sort of warm, protective feeling about you. One doesn't know where that sort of nonsense will end.'

The words were light-hearted but she knew very well what I meant. I knew perfectly well where a warm protective feeling could end, not just in animal snacks, and so did she, and she knew I knew she knew. That was obvious when she leaned slightly against my left side and put her hand on my knee, and said:

'I reckon you're about the lousiest spoken lover a woman could fall for, which I'm not doing, of course.'

'I could improve—in London, where I'll join you for a day or two after this darned Turkish representative has left the island in one piece, if he does.'

She thought it over, looked worried, and said:

'What if *you* don't leave the island in one piece?'

I put my arm round her shoulders and pressed her against me.

'I can look after myself—if you feel an unyielding substance around my left side take no notice. Girls shouldn't tamper with guns.'

She drew herself away impatiently.

'You know as well as I do that a gun is a poor defence against a killing attempt by this lot.'

'It's better than nothing.'

'So's a bag of pepper. And cheaper.'

I became serious again.

'Please will you go. I want you to, not only for personal reasons. So please go, Hellena, will you? For me?'

I meant it. I couldn't go to the British High Commission for radio help. Anybody from Ducane's lot would be as popular, for diplomatic reasons, as a Pope at a Black Mass. She said abruptly.

'Why don't *you* go to see Ducane? I'll go to Athens, if you like, and you go to London. Tell him in person, dictate to a secretary, get it all down with carbon copies. Well?'

'I can't leave now—there's Demirel.'

'Demirel, Demirel, Demirel! What the hell can you do about him now? Nicolaides dead, Ahmet Aksu reporting at third or fourth hand, Alex Ford dead, radio link cut—so what *can* you do?'

She almost shouted the words. But she had a half sob in her throat.

'Maybe nothing, maybe something,' I replied lamely, and tried to put my arm round her shoulders again, but she wouldn't have it.

'Either you can do something or you can't—which is it?'

I shook my head uneasily, because I was afraid to explain my thoughts. Being amoral is dead easy. So is being immoral, come to that. You don't need much training. To be laughed at for old fashioned ideas is more difficult. I was tired. Fed up. Disinclined to be battered by sneers. I tried to side-step her.

'Ducane may try to contact me through some other station on the island.'

'Is there another station?'

'I wouldn't know,' I said irritably. 'Or he may fly another

officer out, who'll expect to find me here.'

'Will that do any good?'

She was sitting bolt upright, one hand on the rock on each side of her, head turned to stare at me. Crusty but dreamy old Frank Baker couldn't ever have coped with her, I could see that.

'Would that do any good?' she asked again. 'Given the time factor?'

'Probably not.'

'So why stay to be shot at—or whatever they'll do to you?'

She had me pinned in a corner now, and I thought, well, hell, if she wants to laugh then let her bloody well laugh. So I shrugged and said wearily:

'All right, I'll tell you why I can't go. I can't go because I'm square, see?'

'Square?'

'Square—not trendy, see? You know what square is? And trendy, I guess you know that? Square is old fashioned, see?' I was being offensively defensive against the sneers to come.

'Go on,' she said coldly.

'I can't leave the station here, even though it's just about non-operational now, I can't do it, I know it would be logical for me to report to Ducane in person, but——'

She interrupted me, saying lightly:

'I know, I know—"The boy stood on the burning deck whence all but he had fled", that stuff.'

'That stuff, square stuff,' I said between my teeth. 'You don't understand, it's old fashioned. I won't let these thugs think I've been run out of place.'

I was wide open for the shaft she shot, but I didn't expect it. She said:

'You're scared that Ducane'll think you chickened out of Cyprus just when it was getting too hot. Isn't that it, isn't that really it, Tom? You're afraid of what Ducane will think?'

I can see now that she was being crafty, to get me out of the place, but I didn't see it then, and I slammed back at her.

'I would think it'll cost me my job,' I said tartly, 'telling *you* everything, asking *you* to fly over instead of *me*. If that's being afraid of Ducane, then you're right, kiddo, dead right.'

She turned her head away and looked at the sea and said:

'Why do it—why ask me to go?'

'I've told you,' I said sullenly. 'I want to get you out of this dump, because I think there's a threat to you, too, and I want Ducane to know the facts, at once, without delay; and thirdly, I'm square, there's this thing, it's something inside you. It's daft, but it's there.'

'Obstinacy?'

I had been filling my pipe, and I took out my lighter, but I put it away again. There was no necessity to pinpoint our position.

'Probably. I've said it's daft.'

She swung her head round again and looked at me, and said:

'Dear old square Tom Carter.'

'One is as one is,' I muttered.

'I said I wasn't and I wouldn't, but I am.'

'What?'

She gave a hopeless sort of sigh and turned her head to me.

'Well—you know.'

If anybody had timed it with a stop-watch, I reckon the kiss would have notched up ninety seconds. This is quite a long time unless there are other complications.

I made her memorise Ducane's telephone number, giving her a key word for recalling it in case she forgot, though I knew she wouldn't. I gave her the money, and said Ducane would lend her more, if needed, and told her to tell the hotel that night that she was leaving at eight o'clock the next day to stay unexpectedly with friends in Famagusta, and she would need a taxi.

As she was driven away from the hotel, she should say casually to the driver that she had changed plans and wanted to go to the airport. At the airport she must trust to luck. But a First Class single day-fare from Cyprus to London is not cheap. She should have no difficulty in getting a seat during the day. She promised to send a telegram to me on arrival signed Aphrodite. It seemed as good a name as any.

So we said goodbye.

So we said we'd meet in London in a few days. Maybe a week or so. And said goodbye again. It's the sort of thing you do, and hope for the best.

Then we parted, with a brief quick kiss, and I watched her walk slowly back to the steps leading up to the hotel. As her solitary figure receded I thought how lonely she looked. At the bottom of the steps she turned, and made a movement with her hand which was a half wave, irresolute, probably wondering if I was still watching her.

I snatched my white handkerchief from my breast pocket and flicked it briefly towards her, hoping she might see its whiteness. But I doubted it.

My heart was aching.

Sometimes it starts with animal snacks and ends in love, and sometimes it starts with love and ends in snacks, and sometimes it takes a long while, and sometimes a very short while. But parting is always parting, and don't let any dumb cluck tell me that parting is such sweet sorrow.

There was nothing sweet about it. There couldn't be. Not in Cyprus, not in those days, not in our situation. I was frightened for her. Also for myself. The old bomb fear was back. I stood for a few moments, eyes closed, striving to visualise every detail of her that evening. In case something went off bang. In case it didn't kill me. In case it blinded me. Just in case. That's what I said to myself. Just in case.

It was a few minutes past eleven when I got back to the hotel and pushed through the swing door. A young couple followed me in, and I held the door open until they were through, meanwhile gazing around without a thought in my head, listlessly, tired and dispirited, until I saw where Ben Cullon kept the oblong box containing his so-called sacred scarab.

Then I woke up all right.

The chiselling, round where the box had been, had been neatly done, unhurriedly, even the bits and pieces of cement which must have fallen to the floor had by now been swept up. All that remained was a dark hole in the wall, an inch or two deep.

I stared at it for a few seconds, then went to the reception desk to collect my room key. Nobody was at the desk. This didn't surprise me. They got casual at that time of night.

My key was not in its pigeon-hole. That did surprise me. I walked up the broad carpeted staircase to my room, slowly, thinking, not feeling tired or listless any more. The key was in the door for me to see and use.

Somebody was in my room who didn't mind being found there. Such as a hotel proprietor checking up on something. Or a hotel proprietor who wanted to talk to me. Even on his day off.

I turned the key and opened the door and walked in. None of this kicking the door open and peering cautiously round. I reckoned nobody was going to gun me down on the threshold.

Saleh Karim certainly wasn't, he wanted to talk.

Chapter Twelve

He tried to struggle to his feet, dark eyed, heavy and unwieldy. I motioned him back into the chair, and he subsided without protest.

'How the hell did you get in here?'

It wasn't a greeting filled with old-world hospitality and charm, but I wasn't feeling filled with old-world hospitality, and haven't any charm anyway. He took no offence, he seemed to think it a natural question. Doubtless it was. He had had the nerve to order some coffee, and had probably put it on my bill.

'Leo, at the desk, he knows me, Mr Carter. I said you were expecting me, I would wait for you in your room. I said that was arranged. He gave me the key.'

'Good old him.'

'I beg your pardon?'

'Nothing.'

I slumped down into a chair opposite him, at the table, and stared at him, saying nothing, asking nothing, giving him no lead, waiting for the opening gambit. It was feeble enough when it came.

'I have the numbers of three passports I shall be taking to Beirut in the next few days, Mr Carter.'

He shuffled his large thighs forward on his chair and handed me a slip of paper. I took it and put it in my pocket without glancing at it.

'Go on,' I said at last. 'You obviously want to talk—well, talk.'

He shrugged and smiled, unperturbed by rudeness, and rubbed the high bridge of his Arab nose. The small diamond in the gold ring on his third finger glittered in the light. My instinctive dislike of him was tempered by the thought of the genuine tears I had seen in his eyes, trickling down his cheeks at our last meeting, when he had read the extract from the book called *The Return Ticket*. It is very hard to hate a fat man when he cries. At other times you can manage it all right, given the right conditions.

My mind was occupied with the puzzle of the hole in the wall where the little box had been, and wasn't any more, and I had a question to ask, but I wasn't asking it yet, not yet I wasn't.

I watched him veil his eyes for a moment, look at his finger nails, and heard him say:

'Mr Carter, I know a Turk who knows a Turk—we go to the same mosque together when he is in Famagusta, which is often. The friend of my friend is a member of VOLKAN, which is a Turkish organisation to defend——'

'I know, I know of VOLKAN,' I said brusquely, and felt a heavy feeling creep over me. Some things make you suddenly furious, others fill you with a dull despair at the stupidity of human actions, at the inability of people to keep their mouths shut. I knew what was coming, I could almost plot out the dialogue sentence by sentence.

I kept a bottle of Cyprus brandy in the room, and fetched it, and the couple of clumsy tooth-mugs they provided, and sloshed a big measure of brandy into each, and pushed one towards him.

'Go on,' I said.

Saleh Karim spread his hands. He said sadly:

'Mr Carter, the ways of Allah are mysterious and merciful.'

I nodded and took a slug of brandy. There was no need to argue about that, anyway.

'Mr Carter, I have heard of the matter of Mr Nicolaides from my Turkish friend. This may break the heart of the girl, Selin, Mr Carter—do you not think this?'

I was thinking that dramatic news travels faster than local newspapers can print it. I nodded.

'She will be very sad. But she is young,' I said dully.

'Children regard some things as the end of the world.'

'Yet the world goes on. So do they.'

'Allah is merciful,' he said, and took a sip of brandy, which is forbidden by the Prophet. 'She is a Muslim, a Turkish Cypriot, she wished to marry a Christian Greek Cypriot, and such things are not good or wise, Mr Carter.'

He went droning on about why such things were not wise, but I wasn't listening properly, I was watching Hellana making her solitary way back to the hotel, stopping at the bottom of the steps to turn and wave, again fixing the image of her in my mind in case something should go bang and not kill me but injure me and blind me so that I would not see her again. But this line of thought was sliding swiftly into another, at first streaked with fear, then also streaked with bands of self-reproach. I should have told her to lock her bedroom door and bolt her windows this night. A poor flimsy defence, but better than nothing.

I should have lent her my tiny ·22 automatic. Not the heavier Walther automatic but the little ·22, which lay in the locked drawer in the table at which I sat. I could have taken it with the money I collected for her.

I thought of Spiros Artaxides and Alex Ford, and the quickening trend of events and felt sick because a voice in my brain was whispering that I would not see her again. Nor perhaps hear her. Nor perhaps feel her warmth. All that would remain to me would be the memory of yet another shadow, fading with time.

The voice of Saleh Karim brought me back to reality with a thud. He had been staring at me with his soft black eyes, and was still talking about the difficulties of a mixed Greek–Turkish marriage both from the religious and current Cyprus angles. His double chin occasionally wobbled heavily, sadly, which didn't surprise me for I judged him to be a mixture of cynicism, opportunism, and sentimentality.

He said:

'The young man Nicolaides was a member of IN-AKEL, that you certainly knew, Mr Carter?'

'I knew he was an IN-AKEL man,' I said carefully. 'That I knew.'

'That also Selin knew.'

I looked at him quickly, but he had veiled his eyes again and was looking at the little diamond in the gold ring on the third finger of his right hand.

'How did you know the name of the man she was meeting?' I asked sharply. 'How did you know it, who told you?'

Saleh Karim shrugged and sighed.

'One learns these things.'

'One learns many things about people,' I said ominously, and leaned forward across the table and looked him full in the face.

'Mr Carter, let us say that a woman in love finds it hard not to talk of her loved one to a friend, and speak his name. Is that not so, is that not true? I was troubled to learn he was a Greek.'

'And you told your Turkish friend?'

Suddenly his thin voice took on a pleading, defensive note.

'I was troubled, Mr Carter—this marriage would have led to no happiness for her, or for this young man. I was worried to prevent it. I talked to her, but it made no difference. She said she knew. She said she would take him away from this island soon and all would be well. She was sorry she had told me his name, she said.'

'She'll be sorrier now.'

I thought of Selin, a girl I had never met, one of the shadows, of Frank Baker's good-natured efforts to help Damon Nicolaides who had served him well in the past; of the furtive, fleeting little love-trysts in the woods near the mosque of Hala Sultan; of Selin blabbing to Saleh Karim, and Karim interfering, and VOLKAN, and the final killing of Damon whom they thought to be not only in love with a Turk but an INAKEL assassin as well.

'He was a Greek, a Red Terrorist, worse than a Communist,' insisted Karim, mournfully, rubbing his nose. 'All would have ended unhappily.'

I laughed outright at that.

'Allah is merciful. Now it's ended happily in death,' I said tartly.

'What will be, will be.'

There was a pause. Then he said gently:

'Mr Carter, I think this poor girl Selin was an agent of yours, even though she fell in love with this terrorist, even though now she may be sad. Perhaps if you wished to give her some money, I would pass it on to her——'

Suddenly I lost patience with him, with the intricate wheeling and dealing I knew he must be engaged in. Ben Cullon had summoned him that evening, just as he had, I believed, summoned Spiros Artaxides. There was something new in the air, possibly involving Hasan Demirel, possibly not.

There was no Damon Nicolaides. I only had Saleh Karim, a poor, uncertain substitute. Yet I believed he could tell me something.

I determined to break him.

As a start, I switched on my radio set and found an item which seemed to be a play in Greek. He watched me with a puzzled expression, and said:

'You wish me to go now?'

'No, I don't wish you to go now,' I replied, rudely imitating his thin voice, and jerked open the table drawer and slammed the little ·22 automatic on the table.

'Now we can talk like old friends, you and me together, can't we?'

He put one thick hand on each knee and half closed his eyes. I could hear his levantine brain rapidly tick-tocking away, telling him that all situations are negotiable, given time. I picked up the gun.

'This thing doesn't make much noise. Just a loud crack—like you could hear in a radio play. I'll turn the radio up before I shoot. You're expendable, see?'

'Expendable?'

'You are worth what you are worth—no more. That's what my office in London says. They don't love you. Who are you working for?'

He began to rise to his feet, trying to look indignant. I put my hand on the revolver and turned up the transistor so that the voices of the Greek players filled the room.

'Keep sitting.'

He sank back in his chair, and I turned the noise down.

'Mr Carter, I am a trader. I try to please Mr Baker, I try to please you——'

'And you try to please Mr Cullon.'

'I live by trade, Mr Carter, without trade I starve, without trade the world starves, without trade——'

His voice grew stronger, as his Arab rhetoric gave him confidence. I looked at my watch.

'Look, this citizen here won't starve without you. To me you are nothing, to my people in London you are nothing, we are no longer interested in your passports, and I'm in a hurry. You'll leave here alive in fifteen minutes, or not at all. Right? I've got orders from London, see? I don't want to do it, but I've got orders. They don't like you any more, see? No love for Saleh Karim, they said. No joy for Karim, Karim is bad news. They know a lot about you, see? Not everything, but enough to make you bad news.'

I grabbed the gun and got to my feet. He looked really agitated now.

'Keep your hands on the chair.'

I walked to the door and locked it, watching him over my shoulder, keeping him covered, more to keep the pressure up than because he was likely to try anything, and sat down, and looked at my watch again.

He was sweating slightly.

'Mr Carter, how do I know—what guarantee have I that——'

'None. You've got to talk and hope for the best. That's your bad luck, isn't it? But you have my word—for what that's worth,' I added grimly, so as he shouldn't feel too cheerful. 'Let's clear up a few simple things first. Right?'

He licked his lips, but said nothing.

After about ten seconds I picked up the gun and reached out a hand to turn up the radio noise.

'What things?' he muttered, and looked at me forlornly. I put the gun down.

'This Mr Cullon, did he ever ask you to search out for him and buy a so-called sacred scarab?'

He shook his head. I watched his dewlaps wobble.

'Did he tell you to say you *had* bought such a scarab, if you were ever asked?'

'Maybe. Maybe not. I don't remember.'

'You often get asked to buy sacred scarabs? You get asked so often to buy sacred scarabs that you can't remember who asked you, right?'

He stroked his chin and I saw a faint gleam in his dark eyes and guessed that Grimm and Hans Andersen were going to have to look to their laurels when it came to an off-the-cuff fairy tale. He leaned forward and smiled happily, exuding the phony old glad-to-be-able-to-help stuff.

'Now indeed I remember! Now I recall all! This Mr Cullon, he obtained this scarab from Egypt in an unusual way, you understand, and because he feared that this Mrs Cullon might worry, he had with me a gentleman's agreement that I should say that the scarab——'

He was getting into his stride nicely. I would have liked to hear the rest of the story, but there was no time.

'Except that it wasn't a scarab, and you know it wasn't a scarab, and you know that its predecessor was stolen, and you know what it was.'

He shook his head vehemently, and snatched a handkerchief from his breast pocket and wiped his forehead. His voice shook when he spoke.

'I was in Beirut at the time it was stolen!'

'Bully for you. You know what happened to Mr Raschid?'

'There was a sad accident on the boat from Famagusta, that I know. He was a friend of mine. Very sad affair.'

I nodded and said: 'Very sad. It looks as though there may be another sad accident.'

He stared at me, eyes wide, high-bridged curved nose tilted up, mouth a little open.

'The second scarab that isn't a scarab has been removed—you saw that?'

He began to wipe his hands with his handkerchief.

'I saw nothing of that! I came in, looking not to the right, not to the left.'

'What is it?' I said sharply. 'What is it in the box that is not a scarab?'

He looked at me pleadingly, eyes becoming moist, lips parted and trembly, so that I almost felt sorry for the poor fat slob.

'You're expendable, like I said.'

He shook his head, tried to speak, failed, swallowed a couple of times, then gave it up. I sighed.

'Expendable,' I murmured sadly. 'Me, I like you, you seem a friendly man to me, but in London they don't love you any more, as I told you.'

I thought for a moment and added:

'Maybe they're right. Maybe I'm wrong to like you. There's a Kipling poem about an old Indian blind beggar called Matun, who when young and fit was going to shoot Adam-zad, the bear that walked like a man, see? But Matun hesitated, because it looked piteous, see, and a fot lot of good it did him, because it tottered nearer, and swiped him across the face, and "he looked no more on women"—and me, I've got a thing about not getting caught like that, and I want to look more on women. So keep sitting. What I've got to do, I've got to do,' I murmured, and reached out for the radio again.

'Mr Carter!' he said imploringly and raised his thick right hand in front of his face as though he could flick a bullet away. Ludicrous but pathetic. I knew he had packed it in now and was nearly on the run.

'Mr Carter, I will tell you a story,' he said frantically.

'I bet you will.'

'Mr Carter, I am an Arab—that you know, that you understand, but some things you do not know.'

'Did Mr Baker know them?'

I let him get up. He began waddling around the room, heavy and cumbersome, face perspiring.

'Mr Baker did not know them. Mr Cullon, he does not know them. Now you shall know them. You will know that I spend some of my time in Famagusta here, and some of my time in Beirut, as did that Mr Raschid, to whom an accident happened.'

He stopped, breathing loudly, and I guessed that this was the moment of truth, the point of no return, the psychological jump between defence and surrender.

'Mr Carter, I am a trader.'

I banged the table and said: 'Oh, for God's sake don't give me all that muck again!'

'My wife is an Arab, my children are Arabs, they do not live in Cyprus. I have a son in Egypt, a daughter in Syria. I have other relations—not in Cyprus.'

He stopped, staring down at the floor.

'This you must know, this you shall know—my Arab brothers are engaged in a just war against the Jews of the unjust Zionist State of Israel. If my brother Arabs ask me to help them, then I help them. That you will understand.'

I gave him a fish-eyed stare and said nothing.

'I am a trader,' he muttered hopelessly, 'yes, I am a trader, but my family lives over there, and if I am asked to help, then I think of my family's safety, too. That is wise, that you will understand.'

'Who asked you to help?'

'I am an Arab,' he muttered yet again, and moved slowly over to the balcony window, and stood there with his back to me. I was watching his hands.

'Who asked you to help?' I repeated loudly. 'Palestinian Liberation Front people, that crowd? Who?'

'Not them.'

'Some group, connected with them?'

'Perhaps, I do not know.'

'An assassination group, a hijacking group?'

'I do not know.'

'Ghosts, I suppose—you've been helping ghosts? You can join them. Pity.'

I made a metallic sound with the jacket of the ·22 automatic. It was not in my interests to kill him. I wanted him to talk. I did not want to kill him, either, not then, because I am not a killer by nature, and it would lead to complications, and neither fear, nor greed, nor rage, nor sexual jealousy was in me, not at that moment.

He swung round, his eyes wide, and he noted my left hand on the volume control of the transistor. Again I almost felt sorry for him.

'Mr Carter, sir, they were indeed like ghosts to me! That I will swear in the name of Allah. They came to me at night, in different places, to talk to me, in Beirut, and I did not know their names, me, I am a trader, but——'

His squeaky voice died away in his throat.

'Raschid?' I said abruptly, going back to square one. 'Why the sad accident? Tell me that, go on, tell me that, you've still got a chance, look, I'd take a chance with London if you——'

He didn't let me finish. He said agitatedly:

'I do not know! That you must believe! Raschid I knew, and him I helped, but not in the matter of the box, that not, not at all. This too I tell you—Raschid, he too, did not know what was in that box, that he told me, that you must believe, he had to remove it and take it to Beirut unopened, that he told me. To Beirut, unopened, and give it to—a man.'

'One of the ghosts?'

'To one of the ghosts.'

He produced a feeble, ingratiating sort of smile, which I couldn't be doing with at all, because I had to keep him on the run. I gave him another fish-eyed look.

'You're not helping much. Pity.'

'Now there is something else I remember,' he said quickly, and groped behind him, and sat down on a chair by the window. A ·22 is inaccurate, and perhaps he knew it. Anyway, the mood to kill him, the rage, was still not with me, though I think I could have killed him, even with a ·22, at that range. I picked the gun up and looked at it, just to keep him happy.

'This poor Mr Raschid, he was told that the box might hold certain information of certain things about——'

He paused, not wanting to go on, realising perhaps that he had gone too far, hoping I wouldn't make him complete the sentence. Some hope.

'About?' I snapped at him. 'Go on—about *what*?'

He couldn't fight that one any longer and knew it. He licked his lips again.

'About this Mr Cullon. Later they got the information some

other way, so I am told, so they tell me, but I do not know.'

I patted the little gun in front of me.

'Look, at this moment you're not talking to Ben Cullon, and you're not talking to ghosts in Beirut. What else did they want to know about Cullon? What did they ask you about him?'

'Ordinary things—his way of life, each day how it was usually spent. Week to week, month to month—same questions. Not about secrets. Just daily life.'

I nodded. For once I believed him.

'You work for Mr Cullon—like you do for me, like you did for Mr Baker, like you do for these ghosts in Beirut, you've got quite a clientele, you have.'

He shrugged, lowered his eyes.

'I do little things for him. As I did for Mr Baker. Passport information. Little things like that. Small things, not harmful.'

'Like selling him a passport in the name of W. A. Anderson? Same name as the man who might have been killed if he'd gone on the plane with Mr Baker and Mahmoud Kadem, the Turk. Only he didn't go, did he? Cullon knew better than to go, didn't he? Either he had the bomb planted in the plane himself, or he knew it was to be planted there—and if he knew, who told him?'

I got to my feet, and shouted across at him:

'Who told him? You, I suppose? How much does he pay you? More than Mr Baker did? Is that it? You didn't want to see your main meal-ticket killed, right? Twenty or more other people could die, but not this Cullon—not Mr Baker *and* Cullon, two meal-tickets in one bang, that wouldn't do, would it?'

I stopped and drew a deep breath, because I was getting worked up, and that's bad. From across the room I heard him mutter:

'I did not tell him. I did not dare to tell him. I did not want him to die, but I did not warn him. I did not dare to. I have my family in Arab countries, I did not tell him. But somebody told him, and now just the same it is difficult for me, because somebody told him, and I fear for my family.'

I believed him, even though he gave a sigh, so deep, so long, it must certainly have been phoney. I stood up and flung the main question at him good and hard.

'Who put the bomb on that plane, who did you get to do it to please these Beirut ghosts?'

There was quite a silence. He had stopped ambling around, and stood a few feet away, watching me, till he again did the old eye veiling act, and I thought something good was coming, because I never knew a guy who could think up a faster tale.

'I know a man who knows a man who works at the airport,' he began earnestly. 'He has much to do with loading tins of food for the meals of the passengers, that I can tell you, that——'

'Name?'

'His exact name is——'

He paused and tried to look puzzled.

'Memory going?'

He shook his head.

'I am an old man, I——'

'You are an old liar.'

He shook his head again, heavily, from side to side, chins wobbling, eyes pleading but watchful, so that once more I felt pity, a remote pity, illogical because he was a rogue, but I watched him warily. The lines about Matun and Adam-zad ran, *'Nearer he tottered and nearer, with paws like hands that pray—from brow to jaw that steel-shod paw, it ripped my face away.'* I didn't remember the words, not then, I just remembered the sense of them.

Later I remembered them, never can forget them, but not then. Even the sense of them seemed irrelevant at that moment. He hadn't got steel-shod paws.

I could tell from the hang of his jacket and trousers that he had no gun, unless it was in a shoulder holster, and if he went for that he was a goner. Even if he just put his hand up to scratch his left armpit he was a bad insurance risk. But I knew he wouldn't. He was not the gunman type. It seemed safe to pity him.

Right at the beginning I said that this story had a happy ending, though it depended upon what you meant by a happy ending, and I said that a little plastic bomb could kill, or maim or blind you, and always in Cyprus, since I landed, I had had this thing about a bomb, and about being blinded.

But I never gave a thought to some acid like vitriol. It's often used. It's silent. It leaves the victim reeling, helpless. To be killed with ease, if desired, even by a cumbersome jerk like Saleh Karim, or just scarred and blinded.

I gave no thought to it, and I did not want to kill Saleh

Karim because there was no rage in me. So I sneered and mimicked his thin voice again and fired another kind of shot, at random:

'I know a man at the airport, too! I know a paid assassin there, and I reckon he'll turn his hand to anything, and I guess he's a pal of yours, and I think the reason London doesn't love you any more is because you are a pal of Spiros Artaxides. You want to choose your friends better, you do, you ask Frank Baker and Alex Ford when you see them in the next world, they'll tell you, they'll agree all right—more choosy, that's what you ought to have been. Me, I like you, I'll miss you.'

I was squeezing the orange, hoping he'd try to trade a few more pips, but he suddenly began to grimace and clutch his chest with his left hand.

'What's up with you?' I asked.

He stood there, muttering and clutching his chest and finally groped in his trouser pocket with his right hand and brought out a yellow silk handkerchief and a short squat little bottle, and gasped something about his heart, and medicine, and pointed to the table where we'd been sitting, and where the glasses stood.

I nodded. I even took a step or two towards the table to help him if necessary. I didn't have any thought about acids.

Why should I have done?

He reached the table, unscrewed the short, squat bottle and tipped the contents into the glass he had been using, and picked it up. I was still hovering around ready to help. I didn't want him to die, not before I'd finished with him, anyway.

'You want to drink that stuff and sit down,' I said quietly. 'That's what you want to do—drink up and sit down.'

He turned away holding the glass in his hand. Reconstructing, I can see why. There was a table between us. He wanted to be close. He could only have one throw.

He stepped back from the table, then a couple of paces towards the middle of the room, and then began to shamble towards me. He was still clutching his chest. His lips were moving but no sound came from him.

As he neared me his eyes pleaded for mercy and understanding. I heard a voice which was mine tell him to stop. But he didn't stop.

Like Matun, the old blind beggar, I had a gun in my hand, but I did not fire though I could have dropped him two yards away. *'I looked at the swaying shoulders, at the paunch's sway and swing, and my heart was touched with pity for the monstrous pleading thing,'* that's how the poem went.

I let him totter another couple of paces nearer me, unwilling to gun down this sad, swollen bladder of a seemingly sick man.

It was then I saw that his eyes, no longer pleading, were fixed on mine. Not on the glass he held.

Not on the medicine.

I stepped back and sideways and put my hand on the transistor radio, and raised the gun so that it was level between his face and mine, and since we were both of much the same height the ·22 automatic was between our faces.

'Put it on the table,' I said sharply. 'Put the glass on the table or as God is my witness I'll shoot now.'

He stopped, hesitated, as I had hesitated to shoot. Then he edged towards the table, and put down the glass.

'Now sit down yourself.'

I watched him lower his big backside into the chair. He never took his eyes off me. He was no longer clutching his chest. But I waved at the glass.

'Drink it—drink it up.'

He stared at the glass, then at me, cleared his throat, said:

'I am feeling better.'

'I'm not. Drink it. Then I'll feel better, too.'

But I knew he wouldn't. By then I knew what he had had in mind. And because I am as I am, it was then, suddenly, that I felt the urge, the sudden hate upsurge, which can end in a killing.

I had never thought seriously about killing a man, except in self-defence; hadn't considered the matter in depth, to use current jargon. I'd visualised the possibility that I might be knocked off by the Opposition, as we politely call them, but not the other way round. And to kill fat old Saleh Karim would have seemed a crime against obese humanity, unnecessary and even counter-productive.

But you cannot foretell the consequences of rages which blow up like sudden Mediterranean storms. Some people have them, some don't. I do, about once every five years. One moment the sky is clear, the next moment there is a red mist on the horizon and native caution, professionalism, calculation of consequences, they get sucked into the mist like peas into a vacuum-cleaner. It is my character defect. I try to conquer it and think I am succeeding. But I hadn't conquered it that night with Saleh Karim.

Now, long after, I feel remorse.

No completely mixed-up character like Saleh, positioned in deadly circumstances, his ideology streaked with fear for himself and his family, and with what he called his trading instincts, should be compelled to face death with the terror I saw in his eyes.

He could see the gun all right, but I couldn't see him clearly, owing to this mist which wasn't a physical mist but a mental mist, and I could see the look in his eyes and it meant nothing to me that I can recall, because in the turmoil of these rages one is conscious of nothing but hate, and in the back of my mind, subconsciously feeding the hate, was the memory of his involvement in the deaths of Frank Baker and Damon Nicolaides, his attempt to get some money from me for Selin (of which I had no doubt he would have retained a percentage), what he certainly knew about Spiros Artaxides and wouldn't tell me, what he had contemplated doing to my eyes, afterwards certainly to kill me at leisure to cover his tracks, while Cullon in some appropriate way would have closed the mouth of Leo, the reception clerk who had give him my room key.

So I sighted the gun in the middle of his forehead, and he turned his head aside and again made the futile gesture of raising a hand to keep the bullet off, and this time it didn't seem pathetic, it didn't mean a thing to me, except that it slightly obscured the side of his head. But enough of his head was clear of his hand for my purpose at that close range.

All pity for Adam-zad had died. Strange to recall now, when I can recreate little but pity from those days.

I had turned the radio on loud. There was a pause in the fierce argument which had been coming over the air, and I waited for a moment till the voice started again, while Saleh Karim whimpered. I think he whimpered. Some small noise was coming from him.

It couldn't save him. Doubtless he knew it.

Then he suddenly switched his head round, so that he looked at me, and I had to re-aim. And he shouted:

'The lady, Mrs Christiansen!'

There was a charge in the musket—pricked and primed was

the pan—my finger crooked on the trigger—when he reared up like a man, and that's how the sad story of Matun went. There was a charge in my musket, and it was pricked and primed, and my finger was crooked on the trigger, but he hadn't reared up like a man, he'd made me pause by mentioning her name.

Chapter Thirteen

'Mrs Christiansen? What about Mrs Hellena Christiansen?' I said sharply.

The rage had gone, drained out of me suddenly, leaving me cold, because I had something to concentrate on, something practical instead of emotional.

'I will do a deal,' I said, 'that I will do, I will do a deal with you if it is worth my while, what about Mrs Christiansen, what about her?'

He looked at the gun and knew what the deal was, he didn't need to waste time asking questions about it. But I spelt it out to him.

'Tell me, upon your Koran, why you mentioned her name, and you shall leave this room alive.'

He looked at me with listless eyes, nodded, reaction setting in, as well it might.

'This gentleman, Mr Cullon, yesterday he asked me to find out the number of her hotel room,' he said, and swallowed.

'Did you?'

'Yes,' he replied in a dull, dead voice. 'I know a man who knows a man——'

'Okay,' I interrupted, 'leave it at that. Skip it.'

I was watching her picking her way back to the hotel less than an hour ago, remembering how I had imprinted the image of her on my mind, in case, for some reason, I did not see her again. I, who'd said I would not fall in love with her.

I reached across the table and took the glass which held his so-called medicine, and tipped the liquid over the shoddy hotel table cloth, and watched what it did to the material, and lowered my gun, and looked at him as he too, watched the acid get to work.

'Why that?' I said softly. 'There are other things—why that?'

'A man must do what he can when Fate is against him,' he murmured. 'A man must do the only thing he can. I am not a man who is quick with——'

He nodded towards my gun. I put it on the table. We both knew the struggle between us was finished, as everything else was finished between us. I got quickly up from my chair and nodded towards the door. I said nothing because there seemed nothing to say. But when he had reached the door I called out to him, asking him why he had seen Ben Cullon that evening. He turned round, surprised.

'It is as I said—to give him Mrs Christiansen's room number. Also he wished to tell me that I should drive him to the airport tomorrow morning.'

Then he was gone, and I tried to ring her, but there was no reply from her room, and they said they could not find her in the general rooms of the hotel. I reckoned that maybe they hadn't tried properly. That is what I told myself as I went down to my car. Nothing had happened to her.

She was all right. She must be all right.

She was still looking cool and fresh in her yellow dress, and the bronze hair around her head was still well shaped and in good order. They just hadn't looked for her properly.

It was eleven-thirty when I arrived, but some tourists were dancing. Most tourists stay out late, or go to bed fairly early in their hotels, but this lot were still on the hoof. The receptionist rang her room but there was still no reply.

I said I would look around for her.

I walked quickly to the room where they were dancing, weaving my way between the thirty or so tables which surrounded the dance floor, looking for a yellow dress and a bronze head of hair, not finding her among people at the tables; then scanning the dancing couples, not expecting to find her dancing, not finding her dancing; thinking she ought to have been there, surrounded by the safety of numbers, but she wasn't.

I left them to their fun, and began to explore other rooms, making myself walk slowly, look unperturbed, repressing the instinct to run about like a guest who has discovered a fire, telling myself again that she must be all right, must be about somewhere, healthy and cool, skin honey-coloured in the hotel lighting; no bruises on her body, none round the throat, dress uncrushed, untorn, lovely hair in order, not dishevelled, no blood anywhere, and none of the signals of death which I had seen when I discovered Alex Ford.

I did not know the layout of the hotel, and opened a door which was labelled General Lounge, and seemed to be occupied by elderly people seeking refuge from tourist noise but unwilling as yet to go to bed. They were all reading books and magazines.

I closed the door gently, and made my way along the passage to another door. This one was labelled Residents Only. It was in darkness.

I found the light switch and stood in the doorway looking round at the empty room, not knowing what to expect, fearing what I might see, for although Cullon had made enquiries about the number of her room there was no guarantee that the attack would be made there. There could be, probably were, alternative plans.

So I stood in the doorway, looking round at the empty chairs and settees, and saw the blue silk scarf by the side of a sofa set diagonally across a corner of the room. Behind the sofa was a tall lamp standard, but that still left plenty of room behind the sofa.

There was no logical reason to walk softly and slowly towards the blue scarf or to peer cautiously round the sofa, but in some situations people don't act logically, and I didn't.

There was nothing behind the sofa, and I stood in the silent room for a few moments to allow my breathing to return to normal, for I had feared what might be there, and I didn't know what to do next, or where to look, and associations of situations and emotions are strange and can leap the years, and as I stood there I had a flash of memory, right back to school and the lines of some poem I had had to learn, *I hear a sudden cry of pain! There is a rabbit in a snare: Now I hear the cry again, but I cannot tell from where.* Something-something-something. *He is calling out for aid, crying on the frightened air, Making everything afraid.* Then some more, and then the two final lines, *Little one! Oh, little one! I am searching everywhere.*

Soppy stuff like that makes Ducane sick. I'm not surprised. Later he said there would have been no question of a chance to cry on the frightened air, making everything afraid. No chance at all. But one is as one is, and I thought of the lines as I looked on the empty room not knowing where to search next. And now for the first time I was seriously facing up to the fact that there was no reply when they tried to put my call through to her room.

There ought to have been a reply, because she was supposed to get up early, and now should either be packing, or in bed, behind a locked door, as I'd instructed her.

So you go to the reception desk and say, 'Look, Mrs Christiansen ought to be in her room. It seems she isn't, and I'm worried about her, and can you get a master key and open her door and see if she's okay?'

Like hell you do.

You know the answers, the spoken ones and the unspoken: maybe she has taken a sleeping pill, maybe she is taking a little walk. Maybe she's not answering because she know you may ring and thinks you're a bum lot, and maybe she's right, too.

I'd tried all the rooms now, except two or three unlikely ones on the other side of the reception hall. Apart from the toilets, there was only the Card Room and the Writing Room. I reckoned she wouldn't be playing cards or writing letters, but I checked the two rooms. Between them was a narrow passage, leading apparently to nowhere. It had no sign on it. I hesitated.

Then I went along it and found her.

The passage led to a sun veranda, and she was sitting between potted shrubs, reading. At the other end of the veranda two men and two women were playing a card game too noisy for the Card Room. They were arguing and laughing. Hellena was looking comfortable and serene. Relief can make you furious. It did me. I could have smacked her face.

Her eyes lit up as she saw me approach and she smiled. She got no answering smile. I flung myself into the chair beside her.

'Why aren't you in bed?' I said angrily. I can see it was an abrupt question for a woman to have shot at her, even by her lover. She opened her big eyes wide.

'I wasn't sleepy. Why should I be in bed?'

Now I knew she was safe I was glad she wasn't in bed.

'You've got to leave now. Don't ask me why, I'll tell you later. Ask at the desk for your bill, say you've got a change of plans for tomorrow, you've got to go to Nicosia tonight—anything. You can pack while they're making it out.'

'Have I got to go to Nicosia tonight?'

'No, but you've got to go to another hotel.'

'Now? This minute?'

'Yes, and will you do me a favour—don't argue about it, just get cracking.'

I put a hand under her elbow and she got up reluctant and thoughtful.

'I've never seen you like this before—hard and aggressive.'

'We're not having a picnic on the sands,' I muttered. 'There's a lot of things you've never seen me like before. Come on. And I'm coming up to your room while you pack.'

I told her what it was all about while she packed, which she did neatly and fast, and we were out of the place in half an hour.

It's been said that British hotels are not run for the guests but for the staff. This is not true of most Mediterranean hotels. You don't get a dirty look if you arrive late at night, and the news that the kitchen is shut and the chef has gone home.

Some two miles out of Kyrenia, on the coast road to Epitikos, I had noticed a large hotel on a hill, standing back from the road, surrounded by trees. I drove there, watching in the driving mirror to see if we were being followed.

For the first part of the journey, for about a mile and a half, there was a car some distance behind. Then suddenly its lights were no longer there. I didn't know if it had turned off the road, or had stopped, and was watching us with its lights switched off as I swung up the driveway to the hotel.

I did not mention it to Hellena. There was no point in alarming her further, and already there was a struggle going on in my mind, and she was the cause.

My instinct was to spend the night with her in a double room, not to make love, but to see that she got away from the island in safety.

On the other hand, I should not leave my hotel for any length of time at this juncture in case Ducane, by one means or another, through another station unknown to me, or another operator, managed to re-establish communications. Or even arrive himself. I couldn't put it past him. I could imagine what he'd say later. He hadn't been able to contact Tom Carter at first, no he hadn't, because Tom Carter had been spending the night at another hotel with a dolly bird.

Furthermore, I hadn't forgotten Saleh Karim's statement that he was due to drive Cullon to the airport in the morning. To meet whom? Some very important guest? Some distant employer? And would Spiros Artaxides once more be around, surveying the scene from a discreet distance?

There was no difficulty about getting a room for her. But when, at the Reception desk, they said, 'Double room?' I saw her eyes look at me appealingly, and there was the shadow of fear in them, and I knew she desperately wanted me to stay.

'Single room,' I said.

The night porter took her bags up. We walked behind him in silence. I told myself that there is no hundred percent security, you couldn't cover all points, alone, guard against all threats, erect impregnable defences against all risks and dangers, not in Intelligence work. Something or somebody must be at risk. One could only reduce the risk.

I had done so. I had moved her from her former hotel to this one. I could do no more.

When the porter had gone, with his tip, and closed the door tactfully behind him, doubtless thinking his own carnal thoughts, I said cheerfully that she would be all right here.

She sat on the side of her single bed, staring down at her hands folded in her lap. She said nothing. I went over to her and caressed her cheek with the back of my hand, and said again:

'You'll be all right here, darling. You must go to bed. And I must get back. I'll fix a car for you at the desk on my way out. See you in London.'

I kissed the top of her head, and moved to the door, but as I was opening it I heard her get up and she ran to me.

'Tom, I'm scared. Can't you stay with me? Or near me? Maybe you could get a room next door or across the passage and I could come and sit in it with you, or you could sit in here. Not even all night, just until the sky lightens a little, just till it's nearly dawn. Couldn't you?'

The plea was groping towards my heart, by-passing the brain, the professionalism, the years of training. I stamped on it, because I had to crush it. I said coldly:

'What are you scared of? Here—when nobody knows you are here?'

'How do I know nobody knows? There was a car behind us most of the way here.'

I thought and hoped she hadn't seen it.

'So there was a car behind us part of the way! So we can't have the highway to ourselves,' I teased. 'That's bad, that is, very bad, but I saw the car. I think it turned off to the right about half a mile from here.'

She put her hand on my arm, and said urgently:

'It didn't, its lights didn't swing round—one moment they were there, the next they had been switched off. I think it was parked on a lay-by near a path leading to the beach.'

'Two young tourists going for a nude moonlight bathe,' I said, and smiled.

But I was thinking of the Volkswagen I had seen parked by the road on the day I had talked with Damon Nicolaides on the headland, and I was thinking of his tense, nervous young face, as if he had had a glimpse of what night happen, though not the manner of it, and now there was Hellena's fear, and I was thinking, too, of how Alex Ford looked the last time I saw him.

'Please stay, Tom,' she whispered.

Now my brain was arguing the other way, telling me to do what I wanted to do, pointing out that to Cullon she was as important a target as me, in some ways, and a more urgent one since she was due to leave in the morning, and would tell Ducane what she and I alone had in our heads.

But professionalism had to win. Professionalism, hitting back, told me that it was better to split up, divide the danger. I spoke heartily and tried to believe what I said.

'Look, you want to get this Big-Brother-is-watching-you complex out of your system, darling, you do really. I've got to go back, be around, see?'

I kissed her lightly and left. At the turn in the passage I looked back. She was still standing by the door. Elegant but forlorn.

On the way out, I fixed a car for her. Then I drove back to my own hotel, noting that there was now no car on the lay-by. If they'd gone for a swim it must have been a quick one.

On the way back I kept repeating that there could be no hundred percent safety, that one couldn't cover every possibility. Not by oneself, not even with other people to help, certainly not alone.

But the thought of Alex Ford kept recurring, that and the memory of Hellena watching me leave her.

It was two o'clock in the morning when I decided to go into Ben Cullon's photographic room. It was a sudden decision, based on a sudden idea, which might have occurred to me earlier if I hadn't been worrying about Hellena.

I had been assuming that he was going to meet somebody at the airport.

Now, remembering that he had ordered Saleh Karim to drive him there—and I was sure it was an order, not a request—I felt sure that this was not the case.

He was leaving himself.

He was not going to be on the island when the blow against Hasan Demirel was struck. He was going to be miles away, maybe in Athens, and he'd stay there to see what happened. Then he'd return, his old gay, cheerful extrovert self.

I couldn't see why he wanted Karim to drive him, and not some hotel driver, but it didn't seem an important point. Not then.

Supposing he didn't return after all? Supposing he took with him, or removed, anything incriminating from his photographic room—if there was anything there. But was there?

I began to waver. There was no real reason to think a break-in would be worthwhile. Yet I knew I would regret it if I didn't go in. There could be little or no risk at that time in the morning.

The idea of the door being fitted with a burglar alarm certainly occurred, and I didn't relish the idea of a jangling bell going off when I opened the door. If it did, I would just cut and run, and be in my darkened bedroom and in bed by the time anybody arrived on the scene. So I certainly thought about a burglar alarm.

My mistake was not to think about one of the more modern ones, which wouldn't set bells loudly ringing all over the dump, which would be wired up under the floorboards and connected to a low toned buzzer in Cullon's sitting-room, or by his bedside, or both.

So I set about things happily enough, assembling the collection of small tools in their chamois leather case, the pencil-point torch, and the black silk gloves. I didn't take the Minox camera. I didn't want evidence to produce in court, I wanted the evidence of my own eyes.

I hesitated about a gun, then decided to take one largely for psychological reasons. It makes you feel happier. The Walther automatic was too cumbersome and had no silencer. I had a very special silencer for the little ·22 automatic, and fitted it on because there would be no radio background as there was with Karim.

So that was that. I went forth happily enough. Indeed at one point during the preparations I softly hummed a few bars of a song.

The difficulty presented by certain Yale type locks is in proportion to the snugness with which the edge of the door fits against the jamb opposite, the condition of the wood, and whether there is warping.

His door was in reasonable condition. But it presented no real difficulty, and I was safely inside in three minutes, though in the circumstances the use of the word safely is unfortunate, since the moment I crossed the threshold a buzzer must have been sounding off by his bedside. The door squeaked behind me as I closed it, and I began using my torch.

The wall by the door was blank, the wall to the left bore some framed photographs of landscapes and ruins which I suppose he was proud of. The windows were opposite the door, and were screened by heavy, light-proof black curtains. The wall to the right was taken up partly by a sliding door, which I assumed was either an entrance to a partitioned section of the room, or to a wide cupboard recess.

I would have done well to look at it more closely, since it led to another room which had a door of its own in the passage.

My torch fell upon the usual equipment of these places—two or three cameras, development tanks, basins with running water, the lot.

There was a cupboard with a sliding door under the basins, and since one had to start somewhere I had a look in it, but there was nothing of interest, and I turned to the floor, which was covered with large black and yellow squares of some material the nature of which I never discovered. I was interested in the floor because so much is so often sunk beneath floorboards.

I was bending down examining the area when I thought I heard a slight sound by the door, and straightened up and took the ·22 out of my pocket. Then there was a squeak as the door opened and the room lights went on, and there he was, wearing a maroon-coloured dressing-gown, looking very fish-eyed indeed and holding a short, squat piece of weaponry in his right hand.

We looked at each other for about five seconds.

I didn't feel scared; shocked, yes, but not scared, it was all too sudden.

'Who's going to fire first?' I said bleakly.

'I am,' a woman's voice said behind me.

Chapter Fourteen

'Don't drop your gun, it might go off. Put both your hands up,' said the voice of Marion Cullon.

I did so and felt the soft skin of her fingers as she reached up and took the revolver from my right hand. Ben Cullon was keeping me covered but he said mildly:

'You can lower your hands if you want to, but slowly and keep them away from your pockets, son.'

So I did so, and recalled the darkness visible I had seen outside, and the interior of a Masonic Lodge, and the reason is simple enough, though I shall not reveal it in full. I know that Masonic ceremonies, the secret signs and passwords, have been shown to millions on television, and certainly in Britain it is all harmless enough. Be that as it may, I swore not to reveal them personally when I was initiated and that's that.

But I can say that a Mason in distress makes certain movements with his hands and invokes a bereaved woman, the mother of one of our legendary Masonic figures.

Now, with irony in my voice, I invoked the words of a Mason in distress. I expected no response. Just as well.

He looked at me as though I were halfway round the bend. Then, surprisingly, he put his gun in his pocket. There were two stools in the room. He sat on one, and motioned me to the other, and said:

'Okay, Marion—you can go back to bed.'

I heard the sliding door close behind me. Cullon said quietly:

'This had to happen, didn't it?'

'Not this way,' I said bitterly.

He shook his head.

'Some way like this, it had to happen some way like this, buster. I guess you and Frank and probably the Christiansen dame, you've been barking up the wrong tree, all of you. And I am darned sorry I had to let you go on barking.'

'Meaning?'

He got up and began to wander round, though I noticed he kept a hand in the dressing-gown pocket where the gun was.

'Let me put it this way—for a start. You had a nasty incident in your room tonight with old Saleh—he's unpredictable that guy. So were you, come to that.'

He'd turned his back, so I didn't see his expression. I didn't need to, and now I didn't need to ask how he knew about a lot of things. I suppose he had more than one room bugged, but maybe the bug in Frank's old room worked better than others. So he'd put me in it. They get tempermental, these bugs.

'I'm leaving tomorrow—as you know. And as I know you know,' he added with a little fleeting smile.

'Job done?'

'Job done,' he agreed.

'Russian KGB pleased?'

I didn't think I had anything to lose by saying it. He laughed. It sounded a genuine laugh.

'You lot, you've got the KGB on the brain.'

He went to a small case standing near a camera, and opened it. It contained a number of lenses and other instruments.

'This case always travels with me. This stuff is valuable.'

He picked out a very small oblong metal box and stared at it.

'This has been worrying you, hasn't it?'

I stared at it, noting the size and shape, remembering the hole in the doorway.

He nodded and handed me the box. That certainly surprised me.

'Open it. It won't bite.'

It had a beautifully fitted sliding metal lid. I slid the lid along cautiously, holding it away from me. I didn't trust him any more than before. You have a feeling when some citizens wish you well. I didn't think this one did.

Inside was a tiny scroll.

'Take it out,' I heard him say. 'Read it.'

He switched on another light so that I could better read the tiny writing. I read:

Hear, O Israel: The Lord our God is one Lord:
And thou shalt love the Lord thy God with all thine heart, and with all thy soul, and with all thy might.
And these words, which I command thee this day, shall be in thine heart:
And thou shalt teach them diligently unto thine children, and shalt talk of them when thou sittest in thine house, and when thou walkest by the way, and when thou liest down, and when thou risest up.

And thou shalt bind them for a sign upon thine hand, and they shall be as frontlets between thine eyes.
And thou shalt write them upon the posts of thy house, and on thy gates.

There was more, but he interrupted me, and I looked up at him in astonishment, for the significance of it escaped me.

'You don't need to read it all. It is a *mezuzah.*'

'A *what*?'

'A *mezuzah.* Many orthodox Jews fix them to the front-door of the home. We touch it, when we can, on entering and leaving, and also our lips, with our fingers. You will have seen Marion and me do it.'

He stopped and smiled and said sarcastically:

'I guess you think it a quaint old custom, you being a *goy*.'

I said nothing, gaping at him stupidly, trying to reconcile the fact that a man who was an orthodox Jew could be anti-semitic, be friendly with Saleh Karim, use those terrible words about the Jews going to the gas chambers: 'Even rats make kind parents—or so I'm told.'

I'd have got round to the answer, I hope, but not for a while.

'I am an Israeli Intelligence officer,' he said, not smugly, but in a hard, cold voice. 'This I am telling you, first because I am going, and second because our wires have been crossing, and it may save you trouble. We are both more or less on the same side. See?'

I shook my head. When I spoke, I believe my voice was as hard as his.

'No, I don't see, there's a lot of things I don't see.'

He took his gun out of his pocket. I think it was a Mauser automatic. He turned on the stool, and laid it on the rinsing sink behind him, and pointed to mine on a ledge where Marion Cullon had laid it.

'Pick up that inaccurate toy, if you want it.'

I took no notice.

Some things fitted in, I was thinking, some did, like Marion cooking their food, their kosher food, and the Saturdays, the Sabbaths, when if possible they did nothing, and the *mezuzah.* He guessed I was totting up the points, and pointed to the scar near his nose.

'That operation was done in Canada, of course—to make me look like an Aryan who could be violently anti-semitic.'

I felt he wanted to spit, as the Greek soldier at the Tekke of Hala Sultan had almost spat at the mention of the name of Mahomet's step-mother.

'Spiros Artaxides?' I shot the name at him suddenly, but I suppose he was expecting it, and other points, too, since he'd had my room bugged.

'A hired assassin,' he said, 'for anybody who could afford to hire him—for anybody who can still afford it.'

'Like the KGB?'

'Possibly. Or anybody else. He's a cunning, clever hunter, like the leopard. And getting rich by it. He'll probably retire soon.'

'Who hired him to try to kill me while I slept?'

He had been fumbling for a cigarette packet. Now he looked up at me, eyes wide with interest.

'Are you sure it was Artaxides?' he asked softly.

'Not sure, no. But I think so.'

He nodded. 'The noise of the fight was recorded—but I couldn't interpret it. I'm not surprised.'

'You're not?' I said easily. 'And I suppose you weren't surprised to hear of Alex Ford's killing?'

He'd been pacing slowly around the room. Now he swung round and stood stock still. If it's acting, I thought, it's the best I've seen.

'When?' he asked.

'Tonight. Garrotted, as I'd have been. Only this time it succeeded. In his own house.'

He turned away. I heard him murmur, 'Poor old Alex.' For a moment he stood looking at the blank wall near the door. Then he seemed to make up his mind about something. He took a deep breath and said, with a new, strange formality:

'Mr Carter, you and Frank Baker have been coping with two Oppositions. One benevolent—me. And one hostile—the Russians. I've only had one target.'

'KGB?' He shook his head.

'Arabs,' he said. 'Especially terrorist gangs operating abroad.'

'Hence Saleh Karim?'

He nodded. 'Hence him. Double-crossing everybody, of course. But he saved my life. I was playing anti-semitic, feeding them harmless bits and pieces of information, getting stuff back, doing quite well. Somebody over there, in Beirut, somebody somehow got suspicious. They tried for proof. You know the rest.'

'I don't,' I said, 'I don't, you know, I don't know the rest at all. Who killed the unfortunate Mr Raschid—Spiros Artaxides, I suppose?'

He didn't answer the question. He said abruptly:

'The *mezuzah* was returned to me—there was no question of getting a new one.'

'How much did Artaxides charge?' I asked acidly, and regretted the question. His face went wooden. He said harshly:

'You are a professional, I am a professional. I guess you should know how far etiquette allows you to ask questions, Mr Carter.'

He took a couple of paces around the room, seemed to relent, and said in a friendly tone:

'I will correct one thing that Karim told you. He denied to you that he had warned me about the bomb on the plane that killed Mahmoud Kadem and poor Frank. In a way it is true, in a way it isn't. In his usual shifty roundabout way he said he had heard from a friend who had a friend in Beirut—you know how it goes?—that it was not likely to be good flying weather on the day the plane would leave. That's what he said, all he said. He swore he knew no more. He swore it was a vague rumour. It wasn't a vague rumour. He was lying, of course, I know that now, but he could swear to his Beirut ghosts that he had told me nothing.'

His voice was sad. There was a bit of a silence. I said suddenly:

'It's *your* conscience that's involved, not mine. You could have tipped off Frank.'

He passed a hand across his eyes, and thought, and said:

'He'd have made Kadem cancel, too. That would have made three cancellations. Two too many—don't you see?—two too many not to pinpoint Saleh Karim, and I couldn't lose him, not then, not at that moment in history. He was being useful. He isn't now, he was then.'

I made no further comment. It was his business, it was his conscience. After a while he said again: 'It was only a vague rumour, you see, just a vague rumour.'

He spoke defensively. I wasn't surprised. I began to fill my pipe. In the end I said:

'Well, they were certainly after your head all right.'

He made a couple of floppy movements with his right hand.

It was the only Jewish movement I had seen him make. At least I thought it was Jewish, but maybe it was just impatience.

'They weren't,' he said succinctly. 'They were after Mahmoud Kadem. Don't ask me how I know, because I won't tell you. But you can believe me.'

I did believe him. Then, casually, I said:

'What about Hasan Demirel?'

I told him nothing of what I knew. If he wanted to play the reticient professional game, it suited me. He was leaving. I couldn't use him, even if I wanted to.

He didn't seem very interested. He said, 'Demirel?' and looked at his watch. 'Demirel, he should have left by the eleven o'clock plane to Athens, if all went well. So my contacts tell me. The talks were fairly successful, I believe.'

I jumped a little at that. *'Tonight?'*

'Tonight. Why not?'

He rambled on about the political situation. He was relaxed now. I wasn't. After a while I yawned and looked at my own watch, and said I must go to bed, and asked him why he was leaving the island. He said it was Tel Aviv's orders. The station had served its purpose and was being closed down.

At the door I flung my last question. It invited a snub. Surprisingly, it didn't get it.

'Did you use Artaxides much?'

I asked it in the tone in which I might have asked him if he cleaned his teeth once a day or twice. He replied at once, in the same manner.

'Oh, yes—now and again. I guess he had a lot of uses—not all connected with killing. He gets around, that guy.'

'He got around to the harbour cafés tonight, too.'

I smiled at him. He didn't wait for any more, he grabbed the challenge by the throat, and laughed.

'You saw us, did you? I was saying a fond farewell to him—well, let's say a farewell, without the fond. Gave him a few bucks. I've got plans for him and Karim,' he added.

I didn't ask what they were. We left the photographic room. His way led past my bedroom. At the door he paused to say goodnight, and did so, and added:

'You wondered why I wanted Hellena Christiansen's room number. Remember? You asked Karim about it. You were still in your let's-hate-Cullon mood. Poor old Cullon! I only wanted to send her some flowers. I hope she gets them. She stayed here once or twice.'

'You could have asked me to find out for you,' I said, knowing I wouldn't have done so.

He nodded and moved off, saying, 'I guess it wouldn't have been tactful, what with you being so cagey about meeting her.'

He came to my room next morning to say goodbye, and confirmed that Saleh Karim was driving him to the airport in his big Fiat car. Afterwards Karim was taking the car to a garage run by an Englishman along the coast near Lapithos, to get a new battery and a couple of minor spare parts for the engine.

That's what he said, and hesitated, and asked me as a great favour to go with Karim, saying Karim's English and Greek weren't so hot when it came to mechanics. I hesitated, too, I didn't want to go, I wanted a rest. But Hasan Demirel was safely away, and I had telephoned Nicosia and found I couldn't leave till the following day, much as I wanted to clear out.

It's sometimes good to do a harmless favour to an officer of a friendly Service. So I agreed, and he said Karim would pick me up at eleven o'clock, and we said goodbye.

I did not see him again.

At eleven o'clock precisely I saw Saleh Karim draw up in Cullon's Fiat. He had somebody beside him. I went out to the car and saw Spiros Artaxides in the front passenger seat.

Squat and swarthy, he smiled, greeting me as though he had never seen me before. Karim took no notice of me at all. He sat looking straight ahead. He seemed thoughtful and unhappy.

I would have been easy in my mind about going alone with Karim, but even though Cullon had made his own position clear, instinct told me not to go with these two. Then I remembered Cullon saying he had plans for both Artaxides and Karim, so I ignored the warning, thinking that Karim was giving Artaxides a lift in accordance with the plans.

But why hadn't Cullon told me Artaxides would be with Karim?

We picked our way through Kyrenia. After two or three minutes I felt uneasy. There was no real reason. I was in the back seat, able to keep an eye on them, and I had the Walther, but if Artaxides were up to tricks he would have taken account of all that.

I discarded my idea that he was there with the knowledge and approval of Ben Cullon, and saw Saleh Karim's face in the driving mirror, and noted that he still looked solemn. Maybe it was embarrassment due to our previous meeting. Maybe it wasn't.

I wasn't going to enjoy the drive.

So I tapped him on the shoulder and said I had forgotten something, and asked him to drive me back to the hotel. He nodded without comment and turned round and drove me back.

At the hotel, I went inside for a few minutes, came out, and said they could go ahead, I had changed my plans, I wanted to go to Lambousa Monastery after the garage, and then along the coast. I would follow them in my own car. They nodded and drove off.

They made no effort to dissuade me from this plan.

Now I began to wonder why Cullon should not have written his car requirements on a piece of paper, in English, for Karim simply to hand in.

Had something unexpected happened, or had he got a hint of something, or had some idea been strengthened in his mind between the time of our parting in the night, and his last visit to my room?

If so, why hadn't he said something, and again, why had he not mentioned Artaxides?

I was puzzled but no longer uneasy.

In fact, now that I was alone in the Rover I was glad of the opportunity to see Lapithos, which is a picturesque little town set in lemon groves high above the sea, and heavy with history. It would pass the day.

Saleh Karim was not a fast driver, and I soon caught up with him, and we trundled along in the sunshine.

I began sorting out what I would say to Ducane.

There had been success of a sort. Hasan Demirel had been safely removed from the island, as a result, I assumed, of action taken in London and Nicosia on Ducane's initiative, based on my reports.

There had been clarification of the suspicions against Ben Cullon. But there was a tragic negative count, and IN-AKEL was still in being; and Spiros Artaxides was sitting beside Saleh Karim in the car in front of me, happy and healthy, thriving on intrigue, a deadly political animal with a bank balance which must be swelling year by year.

About five miles out of Kyrenia there was a side road which led to a place called Phterykna. I noted the road and the signpost, if not the name, and a few minutes later I was glad of it.

About a quarter of a mile past the signpost, I slowed down to put a light to my pipe, and when I accelerated again the Fiat was some way ahead. I was not worried. I could easily catch up.

It was approaching a curve in the road when it blew up.

I saw it swerve from side to side before I heard the bomb explosion. Then I registered the flash and the noise and saw it roll over twice on its side and career off the road, and hit a carob tree, and a second later it had burst into flames, and the flames were igniting the lower branches of the carob tree, and the leaves were curling and drifting down.

I watched the inferno for about thirty seconds.

Then I turned the Rover and drove back to the side road which lead to Phterykna, and turned quickly along it. As with Alex Ford's death, I had no intention of being involved if I could help it. Near Phterykna I pulled in to the side of the road.

After a while the feeling of shock died away, and I could think coolly. I knew now what Ben Cullon meant when he said he had plans for Artaxides and Karim.

He'd had plans for me, too.

I couldn't make sense of it. Nor could Ducane when I got back to London next day.

We agreed that the Israeli Intelligence people were tough, but we'd never thought they were as ruthless as that. Moreover the whole thing seemed pointless and bewildering—or if not the whole thing, at least the last-minute decision to include me in the bomb killing.

For four days it didn't make sense, not that I gave all my thoughts to it, because I was enjoying myself with Hellena, whose last night in Cyprus had been sleepless but peaceful.

On the fifth day I was called to Ducane's office.

He had something wrapped in paper on his desk and handed it to me. I took the wrapping off and saw the little *mezuzah* box; also a note saying: 'I understand you are still alive and well. Here is a souvenir—B. Cullon.'

I looked at the outside of the wrapping and saw the postmark. Not a Tel Aviv postmark. A Moscow postmark.

'They play chess,' Ducane said mildly. 'He had defences in depth. First, not to be suspected of Intelligence work. Second, the cover of an Israeli Intelligence officer if he were so suspected. But he'd got that *mezuzah* curiously sited, it should have been higher up, near the top of the door, near the corner, not at eye level, you realise that?'

'I don't realise anything at all about *mezuzahs.*'

'You should.'

'Thanks a lot,' I said sulkily. 'Why did he place it so low down then?'

'Your guess is as good as mine.'

I was fed up, and I showed it. One can't know everything.

'I'm not guessing about *mezuzahs,* I'm browned off with *mezuzahs.*'

He shook his head.

'There's no need to be petulant. My own guess is that if he'd sited it correctly, and reached up and touched it, even just now and again, he knew he'd be saying to every Jew among the tourists that he himself was Jewish. He might as well have hung a notice round his neck, saying "I am a Jew".'

He meant no harm. He didn't realise what he was saying. He couldn't know that he was near to starting up the nightmare again, or, if not the gas-chambers nightmare, then the pre-nightmare, the humiliations of the days Hitler came to power, the bullying and abuse, the placards round the neck saying: *'Ich bin Jude'*. I said nothing for a few moments. Then I said:

'I don't see why he had to touch it at all.'

'You don't? I do. First he was getting into the part, knowing he might have to fall back on his second line of defence. More important, he was drawing your attention to it without attracting the attention of Jewish people. He was relying on your abysmal ignorance about *mezuzahs.* He had complete faith in your abysmal ignorance. His faith was justified,' added Ducane caustically.

Then, more cheerfully, he said:

'He was your vulture all right. He nearly cleaned the lot of you up, including those who might guess too much, like Artaxides and Saleh Karim. In the event you cleared him out instead. They couldn't tell for sure, see? They couldn't tell for *sure* whether Frank Baker or you had put anything on paper, see? And Helena Christiansen's letter to you asking for a meeting, that made them really uneasy, and they reckoned time was getting short—and they weren't risking things any more. Not any longer, see? So they planned to clean up and be off themselves.'

He sat back and gave one of his frog-like smiles, and said disarmingly:

'This is all *theory* you know. You appreciate that? Cullon himself hasn't been on the phone to me, not yet.'

I wasn't feeling amused. Vaguely, I heard him repeat:

'He was your vulture, he was certainly your vulture.'

But I shook my head.

I was thinking of Frank Baker, and Karem, and the other plane passengers, and Alex Ford, and Damon Nicolaides, and that the vulture had not been Cullon.

The vulture was man's hatred for man, Greeks and Turks in Cyprus, Arabs and Israelis, Catholics and Protestants, North and South Vietnamese; you could make quite a list.

'What are you shaking your head about?' Ducane asked.

'Nothing interesting,' I said, because it wasn't the kind of thought he'd appreciate, and it wasn't even original. It was pretty corny.

'You'll want some leave before you go back, I suppose.'

I stared at him.

'Go back—to Cyprus?'

'Why not? You've got experience of the island now.'

'Experience?' I said angrily. 'Damn it, I was only there about a week.'

He raised his eyebrows.

'Only that long? Then you won't need much leave, will you? I thought it was longer,' he added, and managed to rake up one of his more unsavoury smiles.

Other Panthers For Your Enjoyment

Outsize Heroes

☐ **Henri Charrière** **PAPILLON** **50p**

Charrière, known as Papillon (Butterfly), is probably the greatest escaper of modern times not only because of his numerous indefatigable and finally successful attempts but also because of the prison he escaped from – Devil's Island. Reads like a Hammond Innes novel, yet it's stark fact, every incident verifiable.

☐ **Phillip Knightley and Colin Simpson** **THE SECRET LIVES OF LAWRENCE OF ARABIA** **40p**

Boy Scout hero or masochist. The authors examine the myth in the light of the latest information. T. E. Lawrence may well be diminished in this cool study, but he does emerge, for the first time in the numerous accounts of his ambiguous life, as a human being. 'Explosive – biographical dynamite' – *Evening Standard*

☐ **Jan Cremer** **I, JAN CREMER** **50p**

This roaring, raucous, autobiographical novel of its young author's sexual conquests in Europe and the US is scandalous, sadistic and funny.

☐ **Jan Cremer** **JAN CREMER 2** **50p**

Continues the roaring, raucous account of Cremer's one-man assault on our sacred cows – the opening moves in which were revealed to a disbelieving world in his international bestseller I, JAN CREMER. 'I'm nervous, schizophrenic, sadistic, perverted, and an inspirer of riots', Mr. Cremer admits – and lives up to every word of it.

☐ **Heinz Werner Schmidt** **WITH ROMMEL IN THE DESERT** **25p**

By a high-ranking officer of the Afrika Korps – the inside story of Rommel's vicious fight to destroy the Allies in North Africa.

☐ **William Rodgers** **THINK: a biography of the Watsons and IBM** **50p**

International Business Machines is the largest single corporation in the western world, and its policy decisions may well shape your future. Consider this: £1,000 invested in IBM when Watson started it in 1914 would be worth **£6,000,000** today. This ominous account has delved into every source – except one. IBM flatly refused to give the author any information whatsoever. The reader will understand why.

American Violence

☐ **Peter Maas** **THE VALACHI PAPERS** **40p**

The Mafia from the inside. Joe Valachi (recently dead in prison) is the only person ever to admit belonging to the Mafia and openly talk about its sinister workings. 'Double and triple-crossing that leave Machiavelli standing; and on every page murder' – *Financial Times*. 'Packed with strange and macabre incidents' – *Sunday Times*

☐ **Thomas McGuane** **THE SPORTING CLUB** **30p**

American millionaires reverting to savagery in their private sporting club. 'People play terrible games in Thomas McGuane's club: sex games, power games, death games. He writes with a scalpel' – *Life* Magazine

☐ **Alan Seymour** **THE COMING SELF-DESTRUCTION OF THE USA** **35p**

A breath-catching novel of an ex-GI enrolled for a university course who goes berserk with a sub-machine gun – and what came of it. What came of it is petrifying indeed. This is a novel – the grimmest one you'll ever read. In a few years time it may well be read as a history text. Buy it.

☐ **Chester Himes** **BLIND MAN WITH A PISTOL** **30p**

Harlem violence as a horrific thing in itself – not motivated, but just blowing its top wherever and whenever . . . a product of a horrific environment – and the attempts of Detectives Grave Digger and vitriol-scarred Coffin Ed to cope with it. 'Himes is superb'.

☐ **Chester Himes** **RUN MAN RUN** **25p**

Even in Harlem – where anything goes . . . knifings, muggings, riots, sex in the raw . . . it is dangerous to get in the way of Detectives Grave Digger and Coffin Ed. The running man is never going to be able to run far enough. 'Shocking, violent, sadistic, not for effect but because that is how Himes sees his Harlem' *Daily Telegraph*

☐ **Joan Baez** **DAYBREAK** **30p**

The world-famous American folk singer talks about all the things that make her tick – and they're all concerned with – to use that trite old phrase – 'man's inhumanity to man.' A heart-warming book and – to use another cliché – a 'tract for the times' by a great artist.